This isn't just a silly squabble, over in five minutes.
This is a serious argument. This is us almost breaking
friends. In fact there's no almost about it.
  'Bye,' I say, marching off, holding my head high.
So high that I trip going up the steps and give my
shin a crack. It hurts a lot. Maybe that's why the tears
are pouring down my cheeks.

'Fast-moving and easy to read' *Financial Times*

'The Girls books are unerringly authentic on the
heightened emotions of .. teens' *Guardian*

'Jacqueline Wilson excels in capturing the type of …
behaviour that's unique to teenage girls' *Evening Standard*

www.kidsatrandomhouse.co.uk

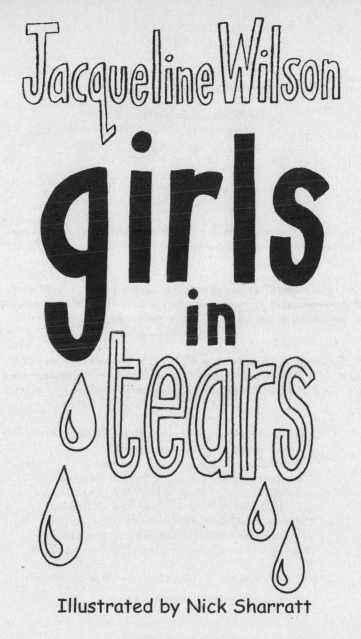

Jacqueline Wilson

girls in tears

Illustrated by Nick Sharratt

CORGI BOOKS

GIRLS IN TEARS
A CORGI BOOK 0552 547115

First published in Great Britain by Doubleday,
an imprint of Random House Children's Books

Doubleday edition published 2002
Corgi edition published 2003

1 3 5 7 9 10 8 6 4 2

Corgi Books are published by Random House Children's Books,
61–63 Uxbridge Road, London W5 5SA,
a division of The Random House Group Ltd,
in Australia by Random House Australia (Pty) Ltd,
20 Alfred Street, Milsons Point, Sydney, NSW 2061, Australia,
in New Zealand by Random House New Zealand Ltd,
18 Poland Road, Glenfield, Auckland 10, New Zealand,
and in South Africa by Random House (Pty) Ltd,
Endulini, 5A Jubilee Road, Parktown 2193, South Africa

THE RANDOM HOUSE GROUP Limited Reg. No. 954009

www.kidsatrandomhouse.co.uk

A CIP catalogue record for this book is available from the British Library.

Printed and bound in Great Britain by
Cox & Wyman Ltd, Reading, Berkshire

For Rosemary, Vicky, Stacey,
Kayleigh, Lizzie, Lauren,
Mhairi, Rupal, Sarah Jane,
Billy, Farah and all my friends
on Ward 27

And this is also in memory
of two very special girls,
Robina and Jo

Chapter One

Girls cry when

they're happy

One
Girls cry when they're happy

You'll never ever guess what! I'm so happy happy happy. I want to laugh, sing, shout, even have a little cry. I can't *wait* to tell Magda and Nadine.

I go down to breakfast and sip coffee and nibble dry toast, my hand carefully displayed beside my plate.

I wait for someone to notice. I smile blithely at my dad and my stepmum Anna over breakfast. I even smile at my little brother Eggs, though he has a cold and deeply unattractive green slime dribbling out of his nostrils.

'Why are you grinning at me like that, Ellie?' Eggs asks me thickly, chomping very strawberry-jammy toast. We've run out of butter, so Anna's let him have double jam instead. 'Stop looking at me.'

'I don't want to look at you, little Runny Nose. You are not a pretty sight.'

'I don't want to be pretty,' says Eggs, sniffing so snortily that we all protest.

'For goodness' sake, son, you're putting me right off my breakfast,' Dad says, swatting at Eggs with his *Guardian*.

'Get a tissue, Eggs,' says Anna, sketching manically on a pad.

OK, maybe it's too much to expect Dad and Eggs to notice but I was sure Anna would spot it straight away.

'There *aren't* any tissues,' Eggs says triumphantly, breathing in and out to make his nose bubble.

'Oh God, no, that's right. I didn't get to Waitrose yesterday,' says Anna. 'OK, Eggs, use loo-roll instead.'

'I haven't got any,' says Eggs, looking round as if he expects Andrex puppies to trot right into our kitchen trailing toilet paper like the adverts. 'What's that you're drawing, Mum? Is it a rabbit? Let's look.'

He pulls at Anna's paper. Anna hangs on. The paper tears in two.

'Oh, for God's sake, Eggs, I've been working on that wretched bunnies-in-bed design since six this morning!' Anna shouts. 'Now go to the loo and get some paper and blow your nose this instant. I am *sick* of you, do you hear me?'

Eggs sniffs, startled. He gets down from the table and backs away worriedly. He's still holding half the piece of paper. He drops it guiltily and rushes to the door, his mouth wobbling. We hear him crying in the hall.

'He's crying, Anna,' says Dad.

'I know,' says Anna, starting to sketch on a new piece of paper.

'What's the matter with you? Why be so snappy with him? He only wanted to look,' says Dad, folding up his newspaper. He stands, looking martyred. 'I'm going to comfort poor little Eggs.'

'Yes, you do that,' says Anna, through gritted teeth. 'He is actually your son too, though when he woke five times in the night with his stuffed-up nose I seem to remember *you* remained happily snoring.'

'No wonder his nose is stuffed up if the poor little kid can't blow it. Why on earth have we run out of everything like tissues and butter? I would have thought they were basic domestic necessities.'

'Yes, they are,' says Anna, still drawing – but her hand is trembling. 'And they generally appear as if by magic in this house because *one* of us slogs off to the supermarket every week.'

I can't stand this. My happy bubble is on the brink of bursting. My magic hand clenches. What's the matter with Dad and Anna and Eggs? Why won't they lighten up? Why can't Dad offer to do the weekly shop? Why can't Anna watch her tongue? Why can't Eggs blow his sniffly little nose? Why does it all have to turn into a stupid scene with Dad shouting, Anna near tears, Eggs already howling?

I'm the teenager. I'm the one who should be shouting and shrieking all over the place. Yet look at me! I'm little Ellie Ever-so Effervescent because – oh because because because!

I stretch out my hand, fingers extended, in a

totally obvious gesture. Anna looks up. She looks at me. She looks at my hand. But her blue eyes are blank. She can only see her boring bedtime bunnies.

I grab my rucksack and say goodbye to Anna and Dad. They hardly notice me. I find Eggs drooping in the downstairs toilet, and give him a quick hug. Big mistake. He leaves a little slime trail on my school blazer where he has snuffled his nose. Then he looks up at me.

'Why are you being nice to me, Ellie?' he asks suspiciously.

It's a waste of time acting Miss Sweetness and Light in my family. I might just as well be mean and moody. 'OK, when I come back home I'll be very very *nasty*,' I hiss at Eggs, baring my teeth and making strangling movements with my hands.

He giggles nervously, not quite sure whether I'm joking. I reach out to ruffle his hair but he ducks. I smile at him and rush off, not wanting to listen to the row in the kitchen a second longer.

Dad and Anna have started to act almost as if they hate each other. It's getting a bit scary. It's weird to think that when Dad first married Anna I couldn't stand her. I'd have given anything to break them up. I thought Anna was all that's awful. I was just a little kid. I wasn't ready to be fair. I hated her simply because I felt she was trying to take my mum's place.

Mum died when I was little. I still think about her every day. Not all the time – just in little wistful moments. I like to talk to her inside my head and she talks back to me. I know it's just me, of course. But it's still a comfort.

I used to think that every time I went on a shopping trip with Anna or curled up on a sofa with her to watch *Friends* I was being grossly mean and disloyal to Mum. It made me feel so bad. Then I'd turn on Anna and make her feel bad too. But now I can see how skewed that sort of thinking is. I can like Anna lots and *still* love my mum. Simple.

After all, I've had two best friends for ever and a day and I don't fuss whether I like Nadine or Magda best. I like them both and they like me and I can't *wait* to show them!

I run for the bus, wanting to get to school early. As I charge round the corner, rucksack flying, I barge straight into that blond guy I used to have such a crush on. My Dream Man – only it turned out he's gay. Anyway, even if he wasn't, he's years older than me and so incredibly gorgeous he wouldn't dream of going out with a tubby Year Nine schoolgirl with frizzy hair and glasses and a tendency to blush pillar-box red every ten minutes.

Oh God, I'm blushing *now*. He grins at me. 'Hi. You're the girl who's *always* in a rush,' he says.

'I'm so sorry. Did I hit you in the kneecaps with my rucksack?'

'Possibly. But I'll forgive you. You must be very keen to get to school!'

I raise an eyebrow. Well, I hope I do. Maybe I'm just contorting my face into a leering squint. 'I don't really go a bundle on school. I'm not exactly the studious type. No, I just want to see my friends.'

'Right. Yeah, I envy girls – they always share so much with their friends. Guys have their mates, sure, but they don't seem to get so close,' he says. 'Oh well, see you around.'

'Yes, see you. And I'll try not to barge right into you next time.'

I waltz on my way, swinging my rucksack. I'm really getting to know him. He's so lovely. A few months ago I'd have been absolutely over the moon, soaring above the stars, pirouetting around the planets, swooping way past the sun. Now it's great, but it's no big deal. He's just a pal. I know he's got a boyfriend – and so have I.

Russell means more to me than the most gorgeous guy in the whole world. No – *he* is the most gorgeous guy, I know he is. I think the world of him. He thinks the world of me too. I know he does. He proved it last night. *Wait till I tell Magda and Nadine!*

I run and catch the bus and get to school so early that they're not there yet! This is the very first time in two and a half years that I've ever got to school before them. This is definitely a day with a difference.

Come *on*, Magda and Nadine! Where are you? There are a few girls in the classroom, the keen ones, like Amna. I wonder what it would be like to be seriously brainy like her, top of the class all the time. But she isn't as good as me at Art, and that's really all that matters to me.

I love Art so much. Dad teaches at the Art College. People say I take after him. I don't like to think that. I take after my *mum*. She was artistic too. I've still got a wonderful picture book she made me when I was little, full of lovely little stories about a

14

tiny mouse called Myrtle. She has big purple ears and a little lilac face with a pointy pink nose and blue whiskers to match her bright blue tail.

I feel a sudden pang thinking about Myrtle. Maybe I can try doing little pictures of her myself. I love playing around and inventing little cartoon creatures. My favourite creation is Ellie Elephant, modelled on myself. I am not teeny-weeny mouse size. I am of great galumphing pachyderm proportions, but I have decided not to care.

I did go on this crazy diet last term and drove everyone crazy too. I was a kind of crazy girl myself, going bananas if I ate anything other than a spoonful of cottage cheese and a lettuce leaf. I certainly wouldn't *eat* bananas, at seventy-five calories per piece.

At *last*! Nadine glides into the classroom, dark eyes gleaming, long black hair framing her chalk-white face. Nadine manages to look Queen of the Goths even in her school sweater and skirt. Though her face isn't utterly colourless today. She's got pink spots on her cheeks. This is the only external sign when Nadine is seriously excited. She struggles to keep her face as blank as a mask – but her eyes have got a witchy glitter.

I wave at her, waggling my fingers extravagantly. She's not looking at me properly. She just waggles her own black-pearl nails back at me. 'You'll never ever guess what, Ellie!' she says.

I can't get a word in edgeways to tell her *my* amazing news!

Chapter Two

Two

Girls cry when their friends say mean things

This is so typical of Nadine! I love her dearly but she *always* has to upstage me. When we were tiny girls and I was thrilled to get my first ever Barbie doll, the standard little-girly version, Nadine got a special collector's Queen of the Night Barbie with long hair and a beautiful deep blue dress. She was supposed to be kept in pristine condition in her plastic case, but Nadine got her out and combed her luxuriant hair and made her fly through the air, deep blue skirts billowing, as she cast wondrous spells and made up enchantments. My own home-spun everyday Barbie couldn't possibly compete. Nadine's Queen of the Night Barbie wouldn't make friends with mine. She said she was much too dull and boring, unable to do the simplest spell. She was only suited to be a servant. So my Barbie had to perform humble and lowly tasks for the Queen of the Night. She didn't like it one bit – and neither did I.

Then Nadine's mum discovered the Queen of the Night had tangles in her hair and a rip in her skirt because she'd been making magic too enthusiastically. The Queen of the Night was confiscated and confined to her plastic palace and Nadine wasn't allowed out to play for a fortnight. Nadine didn't care. She hung out of her bedroom window and wailed pathetically to startled passersby in the street, 'Help me! My cruel mother has locked me up and thrown away the key!'

I was allowed my very first pair of clumpy high heels to wear at the school disco when I was ten – but Nadine came with real pointy Goth boots with spiky stiletto heels. She fell over three times while we were dancing but she still managed to look incredibly cool.

It's been worse since we started secondary school. Nadine had the first period, the first kiss, the first serious boyfriend. Liam is a total jerk but he *is* good looking and he's *eighteen*. They broke up because Nadine found out all the bad things about him – but she *still* seems to think about him wistfully. Until today.

'I've met this incredibly glorious super-cool guy! He's like my ideal dream man, Ellie, just so ultraperfect I almost feel I've made him up.' She raises one eyebrow at me. She does it perfectly. She's insinuating that some people tend to fantasize about boyfriends and end up telling their friends whopping great lies. *Some* people – like me. I got a bit carried away before when Nadine announced she was going out with Liam. Plus my other best friend Magda's so drop-dead gorgeous she can always get any boy she wants. I felt so left out that I started spinning them this tale about Dan, an extremely irritating boy I met on holiday in Wales, making out he was Mr Perfect. Then, when I started, I couldn't stop. Oh, it's such a wondrous relief not to have to do that any more. I don't have to pretend about Russell. And now . . . I look down at my hand. I spread my fingers wide.

'Ellie? Are you listening to me?' Nadine asks. 'And why are you wearing that tacky freebie kids' ring?'

My head jerks as if she's slapped me. I take a step backwards, unable to believe she's said it. Nadine's my *friend*. How can she hurt me so? I stare at her until her white face and long black hair start to blur.

'Ellie? Ellie, what is it? Are you *crying*?' Nadine says.

'No, of course not,' I insist, as a tear rolls down my cheek.

'Oh, Ellie, what have I said?' says Nadine, putting her arm round me.

I try to wriggle away but she hangs on. 'No, come on, tell me. I don't get it. Why are you suddenly acting like I've done something terrible? You *can't* be upset because I teased you about the ring.'

'You said it was tacky,' I mumble pathetically.

'It *is* tacky,' says Nadine. 'Natasha's worn hers for days and her finger's gone all green. I told her she'd get gangrene and that her whole arm would go bad unless she had her finger chopped off immediately. Natasha pretended to be scared and told Mum and cried. Well, she was just pretending, not real tears – not like you, Ellie.' Nadine reaches out and very gently wipes away the tear.

'Natasha's got a ring like mine? Silver, with the little loveheart design?'

'It's not real silver, dopey. You didn't buy it, did you? It was taped onto the front of this new kids' magazine, *Lovehearts*.'

'No, I didn't buy it,' I whisper. 'Russell gave it to me.'

It had been so romantic. Russell came round to my house last night. We're not really supposed to see each other on Thursday nights, just Friday and Saturday, because of boring old homework in the evenings, and Russell has to get up horribly early every morning to do his paper round.

His paper round. So. He didn't go out and choose my ring specially. He saw it in the newsagent's when he was collecting the papers for his round and ripped the freebie ring off one of the kids' comics.

'Russell gave you a *Lovehearts* comic ring?' says Nadine. She doesn't say any more. She doesn't need to.

I don't like her tone one little bit. She's never really liked Russell. I can't help wondering if she's just a weeny bit jealous. Nadine always seems to get wild, weird boys who treat her like dirt. Russell is kind and artistic and intelligent. He treats me like a *person*, a real friend. He's never tried to talk me into going too far with him. Nadine has often implied that he's a bit wet, or even suggested that he can't really fancy me. It's not that at all! He can be *ever* so passionate. In fact, last night it was a real struggle not to get too carried away when we were up in my bedroom.

Russell made out to Anna that he'd come round to lend me his oil pastels for my Art project. Well, he *had*, but then we slipped upstairs to my bedroom. Anna was so busy coping with Eggs and cooking supper and working on the new bunny series for her designer knitwear that she didn't even notice.

Russell and I sat a little self-consciously on the edge of my bed. He demonstrated how to use his oil pastels, though I've actually had similar crayons since I was about seven. Then he sketched out suggestions for my vegetable still life – shiny red peppers next to yellow corn-on-the-cob with deep purple aubergines as contrast. It looked very artistic but I rather wanted to arrange the vegetables into a portrait. I could do a face out of tiny new potatoes with startling chilli pepper lips and mangetout eyes, and then have corn-blonde hair with a bow of baby carrots.

I was pretty proud of this original idea but when I told Russell he was rather crushing. He told me about some ancient Italian artist who'd done this centuries before. Maybe I'd better stick to a straight still life after all. Anna hasn't got any mangetout or peppers anyway. All the vegetables she could find were some big baking potatoes, a very yellow cauliflower, forgotten at the back of the fridge, and a family size pack of frozen peas. I defy even old Archiwhatsit to feel inspired by this sad little selection.

Anyway, I couldn't help feeling a little bit irritated with Russell when he showed me the way *he* thought I should arrange my composition – but I was also very aware of his warm body next to me. I loved the intent look on his face, the little furrow on his forehead, his two front teeth just resting on his full lower lip, the peachiness of his cheek . . . I couldn't help stroking it and he turned to me and kissed me. The sketchbook fell to the floor, the oil pastels rolled right across my bedroom carpet, but we barely noticed.

We soon stopped sitting upright. We just naturally sank down on my pillow, so there we were, lying in each other's arms. We weren't technically *in* bed together, but definitely *on* the bed. It felt a little weird with my girly clutter all around and my old teddy lolling behind us on the pillow. I closed my eyes and concentrated on Russell.

I couldn't close my *ears*, though. I heard the front door slam – Dad home at last, very late. Anna shouted something and Eggs started wailing – not exactly the most romantic of background noises. Then we heard Eggs clumping upstairs, thump thump in his little-boy lace-ups. We sprang apart in case he was about to come charging straight through the door.

He didn't, thank goodness, but Dad might come rushing up if he found out I was in my bedroom alone with Russell.

'Sorry! My family seem horribly in evidence,' I

said, running my fingers through my wild hair.

'It's OK, Ellie. I understand,' said Russell. He started playing with my hair too, teasing a strand out straight and then letting it spring back into a curl.

'It's hopeless hair,' I said.

'I love it,' said Russell. 'I love *you*, Ellie.' He looked at me, smiling. 'Which reminds me! I've got a little present for you.' He felt in his pocket and brought out a tiny round package of pink tissue. I thought *ring* right away. Then I thought, No, don't be so ridiculous, Ellie, of course it couldn't be anything as incredibly exciting and romantic as a ring when you haven't been going out with Russell *that* long and it isn't even your birthday or Christmas. It'll be something sweet but silly, like a chocolate in the shape of a heart or a tiny badge with I LOVE U or a minuscule teddy for a lucky mascot. But it wasn't any of these things. It *was* a ring, a beautiful delicate silver ring with a heart design.

'Oh, Russell!' I said, stuck for further words.

'Put it on, then.'

I didn't know which finger to try. It looked pretty small, so maybe the little finger. Besides, if I tried my *ring* finger Russell might think I was taking it far too seriously, acting almost as if we were getting engaged.

'You put it on for me,' I said.

Russell reached out and slipped it straight on my ring finger.

It meant so much to me. I vowed I would never take it off. But now, when I ease the ring up my finger towards the first joint, I see the skin underneath has turned a dirty shade of green.

'Oh dear, you'll have to have your finger chopped off too,' says Nadine, very gently.

'Oh well, I don't care even if it *is* a freebie ring. It still means all the world because Russell gave it to me,' I say stoutly.

It *does* – but I'd so loved the thought of Russell taking some of his savings and going to some jewellery shop and carefully choosing a special ring for me. It's another thing entirely if he just spotted the ring on the cover of a kids' comic and ripped it off.

'Well, that's great,' says Nadine. 'Anyway, let me tell you about this *guy*. Oh good, there's Magda. I can tell the two of you together . . .'

But Nadine's voice tails away as we both stare at Magda.

Her eyes are almost as red as her dyed hair. Tears are streaming down her cheeks.

Chapter Three

Girls cry when

their pets die

Three
Girls cry when their pets die

Magda never cries. I cry – heaps! Not just when I'm sad. I often cry watching videos. I can even be reduced to tears by cartoons. I just have to think of Mrs Jumbo and little Dumbo desperately twining trunks and my eyes prick.

I cry when I'm frightened too. If a teacher shouted at me in primary school I'd start blubbing. I try not to be so pathetic now but I still hate it when people yell at me.

I cry at sentimental stuff too – little kittens and babies and choirboys singing solos. Nadine sniffs at my stupidity. She hates anything little and fluffy and cute. Still, she can do her fair share of wailing and weeping when she wants. When she finally broke up with Liam she howled for hours and hours. She'd play all these sad songs about breaking up, lying in her black bedroom weeping waterfalls.

But Magda's always so bouncy and bubbly. She's just not the mournful sort. Anyway, she wouldn't want to smudge her mascara. Magda wears make-up every day, even at school (though we're not allowed to). Magda's the sort of girl who'd stop to do her make-up and style her hair even if there were fire alarms blaring like crazy and flames licking at her door.

She's not wearing any make-up today. It doesn't even look like she's brushed her crimson curls.

I forget Russell and his ring.

Nadine forgets her new Mr Wonderful.

We rush to Magda. I put my arm round her waist. Nadine pats her gently on the back.

'What *is* it, Magda?'

'Come on, Mags, tell us.'

'I've killed her!' Magda wails. She puts her tousled head on my shoulder and sobs.

Nadine and I look at each other, mouths open.

'*Who* have you killed, Mags?' Nadine asks.

Nadine herself is always threatening to kill people. She mainly keeps her death threats in the family. Her little sister Natasha is her victim of choice, but when she's in serial-killer mode she mutters darkly about her mother, her father, her nan, even her aunts. But Magda's never seemed remotely homicidal.

'My darling little Fudge,' Magda howls.

Fudge? For one mad moment I imagine Magda attacking a box of fudge with a hammer . . . and then I get it. Fudge is her hamster. OK. *Was* her hamster. Magda went out with this boy Greg at the beginning of Year Nine. He was seriously into breeding hamsters – well, all rodents: mice, white rats, gerbils, anything small and twitchy with whiskers. Magda said his bedroom was like Hamelin before the Pied Piper. When Greg's favourite hamster Honey had babies he offered one to Magda. This was Fudge. For a few days Magda obsessed about her new little furry friend. She told Nadine and me all about Fudge's feeding and toileting and sleeping arrangements.

Fudge did a *lot* of sleeping. Magda hadn't understood that hamsters are basically nocturnal. She expected Fudge to sit up, all bright-eyed and bushy-tailed (well, that's always been beyond her, obviously), ready to learn tricks. Magda hoped Fudge would learn how to beg, to wave a paw, to clean her whiskers on command. But Fudge wouldn't pay attention when Magda tried to train her. She hurtled into the depths of her loo-roll play tunnel and lurked there, refusing to co-operate.

Magda got fed up pretty quickly. She gave up hoping that Fudge had star quality as a performing hamster. She stopped talking about her. I'd completely forgotten she even *had* a hamster.

'Anyway,' Magda went on, 'I sat next to old Greg on the bus and he started chatting me up again. I *wondered* about getting back with him. I know he's not very special—'

'You can say that again,' says Nadine, rolling her kohl-rimmed eyes (she ignores the no make-up at school rule too).

'Yes, but I'm not exactly overwhelmed with

boyfriend opportunities at the moment,' says Magda, sniffling.

'*I* am!' says Nadine. 'Listen, Mags, I was just telling Ellie, I've met this amazing guy. Well, not exactly *met* him but—'

But Magda is sobbing so loudly she drowns out Nadine. 'Greg asked me how Fudge was getting on. I said she didn't really *do* anything. Greg was shocked. He made me feel so mean because I've misunderstood poor little Fudge so dreadfully. I've kept her all loveless and lonely in that cage. It's not even a very special cage. You can get ones several storeys high with slides and tunnels and God knows what, your actual Alton Towers for hamsters, but Fudge's cage is the bog standard basic model, and there she's been, all on her ownio for months and months. Imagine how we'd feel! So Greg suggested she ought to have a bit of a social life. He brought along this very gentle timid little boy hamster. He didn't want anyone too macho to alarm Fudge as she's still a virgin. He said if they got on they could shack up together and Fudge could have babies. But it all went horribly *wrong*.

'We decided to introduce them in neutral territory, so we got Fudge out of her cage and I knelt down with her on my bedroom floor while Greg got the little boy hamster out of his pocket and . . . and . . .'

'And he hated Fudge on sight and attacked her savagely?' Nadine prompts, a little impatiently.

'No, no, they liked each other. Their little noses went twitch twitch twitch. You could almost see a little cupid hamster flying up above, shooting them in their furry chests with dinky little love-arrows. It was so *sweet*. Greg and I knelt together watching them, feeling like proud parents. It was like the romance in the air was catching. Well, I must admit I took hold of Greg's hand, but it was just in a matey kind of way. Then he kissed me. Well, he's learned much *more* about kissing. He's more subtle. He used to attach himself to my lips like a vacuum cleaner and positively *hoover—*'

We burst out giggling – even Magda herself, though her eyes are still brimming with tears.

'And?' says Nadine. 'You got so carried away that you lay down and squashed little Fudge and her furry friend into pancakes?'

'Do you always have to be so ghoulish, Nadine?' says Magda. 'No! But it was almost as bad. Like I said, we got really carried away, Greg and me—'

'You didn't *do* it?' I say.

Nadine stops fidgeting and stares at Magda. '*Did* you, Mags?'

'Of course not, you idiots! What do you think I am, mad? Greg's still a grubby little schoolboy, even if he *is* a good kisser. I want my first time to be really really special, with someone who'll make it romantic and beautiful, someone who loves me . . .'

I think about this very carefully.

'Someone grown-up and responsible,' says Magda.

I nod, sighing.

We have all been side-tracked. We return to thinking of the romance between two young and very irresponsible rodents – a very short-lived romance, obviously.

'When I eventually pushed Greg away I looked round to see how little Fudge was getting on, but she wasn't *there*. Greg's little boy hamster was there, looking a bit shifty, like he'd got his paw over and was now wanting to go and join his mates and boast. Fudge had vanished altogether.

'Greg and I crawled round on our hands and knees calling for her. Greg even wriggled right under the bed and came back clutching this pair of pink knickers I'd lost ages ago. *I* didn't half go pink then. But there was no sign of Fudge. I saw that my bedroom door was just a teeny bit open — and my heart sank.

'Greg put his hamster in his pocket and we went looking for Fudge, right along the landing, in Mum and Dad's bedroom, in all my brothers' bedrooms. *Not* a joyful experience — they're all knee-deep in junk and dead smelly. God knows what we'd find under *their* beds. Then we got to the top of the stairs and I looked down and—'

'Oh no,' I say.

'Yes,' sobs Magda. 'There was this sad little furry huddle right at the bottom.'

'Maybe Fudge thought she was a lemming. They hurl themselves off cliffs, don't they?' says Nadine.

'Shut up, Nadine,' I say, rocking Magda.

'I don't think she *meant* to do it. She just didn't look. One minute she was scampering along the landing, probably in a bit of a daze, having just had her first relationship, wondering if he'd ever call her again or if she was just a one-night stand. Then suddenly she ran out of carpet under her paws, and she started hurtling down and down and down. I hoped against hope she'd still somehow be alive but when I picked her up her poor little head was all floppy and it was obvious she'd broken her neck.'

'Well, at least it was a quick way to go,' I say.

'So, what have you done with her body?' asks Nadine with interest.

'*Nadine!*' I say. I know she's a Goth but sometimes she's way too ghoulish.

'I've put her in my best Pied à Terre shoe box,' Magda says solemnly. 'I thought I'd bury her in the garden today.'

'Great! Then we can have a funeral after school, right?' says Nadine. 'We'll all wear black and I'll compose a sad hamster requiem and you can read a poem in Fudge's memory and we'll paint the shoe box to look like a coffin. Ellie, you can design a little portrait to put under plastic and stick onto Fudge's gravestone.'

Magda is keen on the idea.

'We can have funeral baked meats, whatever they are. They don't have to be real meat, do they? Let's have black food! We could have very rich dark chocolate cake, which looks almost black, and black cherry cheesecake too. And we could raise a champagne flute of Coke in fond memory of poor little Fudge,' I suggest.

Then I remember. 'Oh bum! I can't. I'm seeing Russell.'

'We can have the funeral straight after school,' says Nadine.

'No, he's coming to meet me *from* school. I'm going back to his place.'

'You can do that any old day, Ellie. But we'll have

to have Fudge's funeral now or she'll start to decompose,' says Nadine.

Magda gives a little whimper.

'Yeah, look, you're upsetting Mags. Don't friends come before boys? That's what you're always drumming into us,' says Nadine.

'It's different with Russell. He's not any old boy. It's getting serious,' I say, going pink. I look down at my ring.

Magda notices at last. She gasps. 'Russell's given you a *ring*, Ellie?' she says.

'Yeah, off a kids' comic,' says Nadine nastily.

'I don't care where he got it from. It's the sentiment that counts,' I say loftily. 'I like my ring better than the biggest diamond.'

I twist it proudly round and round my finger, trying not to let the ugly green mark show.

I can't help thinking Nadine is stained metaphorically green with jealousy. It's probably because her relationship with Liam didn't last. Russell and I are in love. We are going to go out for ever and ever.

Chapter Four

Four
Girls cry when they hate the way they look

Russell is waiting for me outside our school. I spot him the minute Magda, Nadine and I set foot in the playground. Russell waves and I wave back self-consciously. Lots of girls are staring. I feel silly with everyone looking, but proud too. I'm thrilled that I've actually got a real boyfriend meeting me. He looks great too, even in his school uniform.

I feel especially ultra-hideous in mine. Despite all my efforts to look cool I've got paint all down my sweater and my skirt's all crumpled and my shoes are muddy from taking a short cut across the playing field to the Art huts. And I couldn't find any unladdered tights this morning so I'm wearing childish socks that ruck around my ankles.

Loads of Year Nine girls are peering at Russell, eyeing him up and down, seemingly impressed.

Magda and Nadine do *not* look impressed.

'Why don't you get him to have a haircut, Ellie? That flopping-in-the-eyes style is *so* last year,' Magda says snippily.

'Are you sure he's really Year Eleven? He looks much younger,' says Nadine. 'I'd never feel kind of *right*, going out with a schoolboy.'

I know they're both just winding me up. They're not really serious. But it gets to me all the same. 'I think Russell's hair is fantastic. I'd hate it if he cut it,' I say. 'And I think he looks at least sixteen. How old is this wonderful new guy of yours, Nadine?'

'*What* new guy?' says Magda.

Nadine looks mysterious. She taps her nose. 'Ah! So you suddenly both want to know. Well . . . he's nineteen!'

'Oh, Naddie! Look, didn't you learn your lesson with Liam?' I groan.

'Ellis isn't a silly loser like Liam,' Nadine says.

'*Ellis?*'

'Yeah, Ellis Travers. Cool name, or what?'

'So why is this ultra-cool nineteen-year-old Ellis wanting to go out with a schoolgirl in Year Nine?' I say. 'As if I couldn't guess!'

'Guess all you like, Ellie, I don't care.'

I care, though. Russell is frowning at me, exaggerating his waves. He's obviously wondering why I'm not rushing over to him straight away. But I feel I've got to find out about this new guy of Nadine's. She's so infuriating. Why does she *do* this to me?

'Is he really nineteen, Nad?' Magda asks.

I can tell she's irritated too. She's the prettiest.

She's the one who should have heaps of boys desperate to go out with her. But all she's got is an on/off relationship with Greg, while I've got a proper boyfriend and now Nadine has got a guy of nineteen—

'He's only five years older than me. It's no big deal,' says Nadine airily.

I hate it that Nadine and Magda are fourteen now. I'm still stuck at thirteen, which seems sooo much younger. And in my school uniform I know I don't look a day over *twelve*.

'Ellie!'

Russell is yelling at me now. I'll have to go. But Nadine is going round to Magda's for Fudge's funeral service. She'll tell Magda all about this Ellis. I can't stand it if Nadine and Magda tell each other secrets and I'm left out.

I stand there, dithering. Russell gives me one last angry look. He jumps down from the school wall, about to stride off. I have to rush after him. I give Magda a quick kiss to apologize for my non-attendance at the funeral. I give Nadine a kiss too to remind her we've been soul sisters since we were in nursery school and smeared pretend red Smartie blood over our wrists and that *I* need to be in on things when she tells all about this Ellis.

Ellis! I thought Russell was posh enough. I am a bit fussed about meeting his dad. They live on the other side of town. The posh side. Those houses cost a fortune. OK, Russell and his dad and Cynthia, his dad's girlfriend, just live in the garden flat but it's still pretty fantastic.

Russell doesn't even look round when I call after

him. I have to run like crazy in my clumpy school shoes to catch him up.

'Hey, Russell, *wait*! What's up?' I have to hang onto his arm before he'll stop.

'Oh, *Ellie*! Goodness! I'm visible now, am I?' he says, dead sarcastic.

'What are you on about? Why did you rush off without me? We're going to your place, aren't we?'

'Well, *I* thought so — but you seemed more interested in hanging about with your friends, having a lengthy natter for half an hour.'

'Half an hour! Don't be daft. Half a minute, more like!'

'But you can gab away to them all day long at school.'

'We don't *gab*. Look, Russell, they're my *friends*.'

'I don't know what you see in them. That Nadine looks like she hangs upside down in a bat cave — and as for *Magda*!'

'What about Magda?' I say sharply.

'Well, she looks so *obvious* — all that make-up and stuff, and her . . .' Russell gestures at his chest with a roundabout motion.

'She isn't wearing any make-up today and she can't help her figure, you nut. I wish I looked like Magda.'

'I'm glad you don't. I like you just the way you are, Ellie,' says Russell, looking at me properly at last. He looks down at my hand. 'Still wearing my ring?' he asks softly.

'Of course I am. I'm never going to take it off,' I say.

I *can't* confront him about the kids' comic. It

doesn't matter anyway. I wouldn't care if it was made out of silver paper. I love it because I love Russell. It's such a relief he's not cross any more. He puts his arm round my shoulders, giving my cheek a quick kiss. Some idiotic Year Seven girls run past giggling and wolf-whistling but I try to ignore them, though I know I'm blushing!

'You've got lovely skin,' says Russell. 'I love your rosy cheeks.'

The whole world turns pink. Russell doesn't mind that I blush like a fool. He *likes* it. I *haven't* got lovely skin. Nasty little spots erupt all over the place, and my nose is so naturally shiny you could use it as a mirror, though I've powdered it quickly in the cloakrooms (plus dabbed on more deodorant, tugged a brush through my hair and cleaned my teeth).

We walk along companionably, Russell keeping his arm round my shoulders. I fit snugly under his armpit.

'You're so little, Ellie,' he says, giving me a squeeze.

I love being called little too. It makes me feel all weeny and cute and elfin instead of a dumpy roly-poly dwarf. I love love love having Russell for a boyfriend. We've been going out together for weeks and weeks and yet I can still barely believe my luck. I finger my ring. Maybe we'll stay going out together for months and months, then years and years, and one day change the ring for a real one.

I've never felt like this before, never never never. Russell isn't exactly my *first* boyfriend, but daft dopey old Dan doesn't really count. We were never much more than mates. We did kiss a bit, but nothing more. I suppose we had a few laughs together, but I never felt this swooping dizzy happiness. My lips can't stop stretching into a smile and I sing Russell's name inside my head at every step.

He's my soul mate, my other half. I hadn't realized up till now how *lonely* I've been. Ever since my mum died I've felt this emptiness inside. I've got Dad, of course, and I love him. I love Anna now. I *even* love Eggs. But it's not the same. I've got Nadine and Magda, and they'll always always always be my very best friends – but they're not the same as a *boy*friend. We can have a great girly time together, but my heart doesn't pound if Nadine puts her arm round me, my pulse doesn't throb at the sound of Magda's voice. I love them both, but I'm not *in* love with them.

I can understand Russell getting fed up because I spend so much time with them. But he's only got to look at me to see he comes first. First and last and all the stages in between.

I snuggle closer still and he kisses the top of my head.

'Sorry I was all huffy with you, Ellie,' he whispers.

'Sorry I kept you hanging about,' I say.

'Come on, let's get over to my place,' says Russell. He gives me a little hug. 'Dad and Cyn will be at work, so we'll have it all to ourselves for a good hour or so.'

My heart beats faster and faster and faster . . .

Chapter Five

Five
Girls cry when
people copy their ideas

Russell's flat is beautiful. It's so big our whole house could fit inside it and it's utterly *pristine*. There are huge cream sofas without a spot on them, Bohemian glass arranged on shelves in precise formation, and even the glossy magazines on the coffee table are laid out with geometric precision. If Russell's dad and his girlfriend Cynthia ever have any children they are in for a big shock. If we let Eggs loose in this room for ten minutes heaven only knows what havoc he'd wreak.

'It's beautiful,' I say politely, setting my grubby rucksack gingerly on the pale carpet.

'It's boring, like a display in a furniture shop,' says Russell. 'It's not a *home*.'

Just for a moment he stops being my big boyfriend who's two years ahead of me at school.

He looks like a lonely little kid, his head hanging down, his hair falling in his eyes. I go to him and put my arms round him. I just want to comfort him, to show him I know what it feels like having to fit in with your dad's girlfriend.

He misinterprets my gesture. His hands go round my waist and he pulls me tightly against him and starts kissing me. His hands are in my hair, his finger stroking my ear, and then he very gently nibbles the lobe and starts kissing my neck down at the very sensitive part where it meets my shoulders. Then his hands are carefully unbuttoning my school shirt . . .

'No! Don't, Russell. Don't do that, please don't.'

It feels so wonderful – but I'm a bit scared. I don't want to go too far. And what if Russell's dad or Cynthia comes home early and discovers us thrashing around on their splendid cream sofa?

'We could go to my room,' Russell whispers in my ear.

'No! Look, I've told you . . . I don't want to.'

'You *do* want to,' says Russell.

'Yes, OK, of course I do – but I'm still not going to.'

'Even though we love each other?' Russell says, taking my hand and kissing the ring on my finger.

'Even so,' I say, wriggling away from him and trying to smooth my clothes and compose myself, though I'm hot and trembling and I love him so much that I don't want to be sensible in the slightest . . .

I do go to his room. I say it's just because I want to see what it's like. It's fascinating, not scrubby schoolboy at all – no mess of old socks and tacky mags and congealed snacks. Russell's room is ultra-hip and cool, with cream blinds and dark brown carpet and a guitar and a soul singer poster. He's got a fantastic sloping desk and high white stool with a spotlight overhead, and the most amazing paints and pastels and coloured pencils and a stock of sketchpads and drawing books and some sweet working drawings of a little cartoon elephant. It's a variation of my own little Ellie Elephant, which I draw all over my school jotter and squiggle beside my name when I write letters.

'It's my Ellie Elephant!'

'Well, it's *an* elephant,' says Russell.

There's a pink leaflet paperclipped to the top drawing. I have a peer at it, though Russell is trying to pull me away, lifting my hair and kissing my neck insistently. It's an Art competition for children, but there's a section for teenagers too. You have to invent your own cartoon character. The winner has a proper animation made of their work and it will maybe be shown on television. And Nicola Sharp is one of the judges! She's my all-time favourite children's illustrator – I love her Funky Fairy books.

'Oh wow, Russell! Why didn't you tell me about the competition? I want to go in for it too.'

'You're too late, Ellie. It's past the closing date. I've already sent mine off.'

'So what cartoon character did you invent?'

'Well, obviously . . .' says Russell, indicating all the little elephants.

'But that's *my* character!' I say.

'No it isn't. You draw your Ellie Elephant with

much bigger ears, and you don't do the trunk so wrinkly, and the expression's totally different.'

'Not really. Look, that's *exactly* how I do my Ellie Elephant when she's happy, sort of kicking her leg up sideways and her trunk high in the air,' I say, stabbing at his drawing pad with my finger.

'Well, that's the way *all* happy elephants look,' says Russell. He taps me gently on the nose. 'Don't go all huffy, Ellie. You don't have the copyright on all cartoon elephants.'

He tries to kiss me and I eventually respond, but nowhere near as enthusiastically as before. He's stolen my Ellie Elephant from me. She's *mine*. I feel like a toddler and someone's snatched my favourite cuddly toy. I know I'm being childish but I'm nearly in tears. It seems so sneaky of him to have kept quiet about this competition. We could have worked on it together. But I don't want to do that now. I'm going to go in for the competition myself. And I'm not conferring with Russell. I'm not even going to tell him.

Russell tries to get me to lie down with him on his dark brown bed but the mood has gone. It's his turn to go a bit huffy. Still, he quite likes it when I have a good peer at all the books on his shelves. He's got lots of Art books, well-thumbed Harry Potters and Philip Pullmans, all the Discworlds, *The Lord of the Rings*, several Stephen Kings, some Irvine Welsh and Will Self but also old tattered Thomas the Tank Engines. When I have a little nose in his cupboard I find several tattered teddies and a tiny army of toy soldiers in the woolly dungeon of his sweater drawer.

We're actually in the middle of a complicated war game, with the toy soldiers spread out all over the carpet, when Cynthia gets in from work. I think she's *lovely* – very glamorous even though she's getting on a bit, with red hair and a smart cream suit and a lot of gold jewellery. She tries *so* hard, fixing us proper coffee and special American brownies, asking all sorts of questions, trying to keep the conversation going. I do my best but Russell barely bothers to grunt his replies.

I wonder if I was as bad as this when Anna first came to live with Dad? Maybe I was *worse*. It must have been hell for Anna, especially when she was only a student herself. I'm going to try harder to help her. She's working too hard with her knitwear designs and Dad's being the typically unreconstructed male, grumbling and groaning and acting up worse than Eggs.

So I'm chatty with Cynthia and help her start preparing the supper. Russell acts annoyed, wanting me to play around on his computer with him. He says he'll teach me how to do all these fancy graphics. He always wants to *teach* me stuff. If he knows it all, why does he steal *my* Ellie Elephant?

No, that's mean. As if it really matters anyway. All that matters is that I love Russell and he loves me. When Russell calls from the living room for the third time I get up to go to him, though I raise my eyebrows at Cynthia.

'I'd better go and see what he's on about,' I say apologetically.

'I know,' she says, smiling wryly. 'They snap their fingers and we're silly enough to jump.'

Still, when Russell's dad gets home it's obvious who's in charge in their relationship. Cynthia's all sweet girly charm and acts like she'll do whatever he says, but somehow she gets *her* choice of wine, *her* favourite programme on the television, and *he's* the one who takes over the cooking of the meal.

I'm fascinated. I wonder if Russell is going to end up like his dad. They certainly *look* like each other. Brian, Russell's dad, has got the same fair floppy hair, the same direct gaze, the same stance, the same walk – he's just a bit more lined and jowly and a stone or two heavier.

Brian calls me into the kitchen, asking me all sorts of stuff, laughing and joking, almost flirting with me, which feels a bit weird. Russell isn't very happy about this either and comes out to get me. Brian takes his time with the meal, but it's marvellous when it's eventually served. We start with fresh figs and Parma ham, then there's a big pasta dish with all sorts of seafood, and then a proper crème brûlée pudding. My dad can cook but his speciality is your basic spag bol. He certainly doesn't do any fancy stuff.

There is also wine, and I get a glass! OK, not a very *big* glass, but it's lovely to be given it all the same. It's such a grown-up meal. Our meals at home aren't a bit like this, mostly because Eggs is always yelling with his mouth full and slurping his orange juice and waving his knife and fork around and spilling stuff all over the place. We don't really talk properly at mealtimes, not to discuss stuff. Brian and Russell have this long involved conversation about politics, for God's sake. I get a bit anxious. I feel I should have my say too, but if I'm totally honest I have to admit I don't know a thing about politics. I mean, I'm into saving the environment and whales and whatever and obviously I want world peace and respect for everyone regardless of race, religion or sex, but I'm well aware that my political thoughts are as woolly as one of Anna's jumpers.

Cynthia talks about equal rights for women and their changing role in the modern world. She asks me what I want to do when I leave school. I say I want to go to Art School just like Russell. I quickly see this is a *big* mistake. Brian goes on about this being a complete waste of time and why should anyone spend three or four years daubing paint about and what on earth did that qualify you to do? You'd just end up teaching Art yourself.

'Ellie's dad teaches at the Art College,' Russell says sharply.

Brian looks embarrassed. 'I'm sorry, Ellie. I wish I hadn't said all that now.'

'It's OK. That's exactly what my dad says too,' I say.

'What about your mum?'

I swallow. 'Well, my real mum died ages ago. She actually met my dad at Art School. So did Anna. She's my stepmum. She *isn't* a teacher. She designs jumpers for children. She started off designing just for this magazine but she's diversifying now, doing all sorts of stuff for other people – woolly toys, adult knitwear, whatever.'

'Where does she sell her knitting? Craft fairs?' Brian asked.

'Oh no, she sells through shops. Special children's shops mostly. There was an article about her in last week's *Guardian*, and one of her jumpers was in a feature on children's fashion in *Harper's*,' I tell them, slightly resenting the craft fair remark.

Cynthia gets very excited and runs and finds her last month's *Harper's*, flicking through until she discovers Anna's little deckchair jumper with all these baby bunnies sunbathing and eating carrots like ice-cream cones.

'I love it! It's so cute! And she's now doing an adult range? I'd like one for me for holidays.'

Even Brian seems impressed that Anna's designs are in the papers and glossy magazines. I suppose it *is* impressive. Anna's become successful so quickly. You'd think Dad would be more thrilled. I suppose it's a bit unsettling for him. *He's* always been the professional – he used to teach Anna, for goodness' sake. And yet he's stayed a teacher, whereas Anna is a real designer . . . Is that why he's being so grumpy with her nowadays? Is Dad simply *jealous*?

Chapter Six

Girls cry when

things go wrong
at home

Six
Girls cry when things go wrong at home

It's very late when Brian drives me back home. I'm a bit scared that Dad will be furious because it's a school night. I take a deep breath when I let myself in. I wait for Dad to come pounding out into the hall, shouting at me. Nothing happens. I find Anna sitting all by herself in the living room. She's not sketching or doing little cross-stitch calculations or knitting up samples. She's not reading or listening to music. The television isn't on. She's just sitting, staring into space.

'Anna?'

She blinks at me as if she can hardly see me. 'Hello, Ellie,' she says in a tiny voice.

'Anna, what is it? What's wrong?'

'Nothing. I'm fine. Well, did you have a good time round at Russell's?'

Normally I'd want to launch into a long girly discussion about Russell and his flat and Russell and his stepmother and Russell and his dad and Russell Russell Russell. If my mouth had a word-count then Russell would definitely come out tops. But for once I need to talk about someone else.

'Never mind Russell,' I say firmly. 'What's up? Where's Dad?'

'I don't know,' says Anna – and she suddenly bursts into tears.

I sit down beside her and put my arms round her. Anna sobs desperately on my shoulder. She's usually such a controlled and coping person that it's scary seeing her let go like this. I'm trying to be calm and comforting to help her but my heart is thumping and all sorts of fears are flying around inside my head like little black bats.

'He didn't come home from the college. I phoned his office but there's no one there. Then I phoned his mobile but it's switched off,' Anna weeps.

'Do you think he's had an accident?' I whisper. In my head I see Dad lying in a coma on a hospital bed while doctors and nurses struggle to revive him.

'I don't think so. He'd have his wallet and diary with him. Someone would have found my name and number and phoned me,' says Anna.

'Then where *is* he?' Dad's sometimes late back home. He takes it into his head to go out for a drink or two with his students and sometimes they add up to three or four or more. But the pubs will be shut now. It's nearly half past eleven. What's he *doing*?

I see another picture of Dad in my head. He's in bed again – but this time he's with a young pretty student . . .

I shake my head to get rid of the image. Anna has her hand over her mouth, her eyes agonized. The same picture's in her head too.

'Maybe there's some crisis with one of the students? Personal problems?' I suggest desperately.

Oh yes, Dad's getting personal with one of the students all right. A tear rolls down Anna's cheek. I find a tissue and dab at her gently.

'Don't, Anna, please. I can't bear it,' I whisper.

'*I* can't bear it,' Anna says, wrapping her arms round herself, rocking as if she's in terrible pain. 'How can he do this to me, Ellie? He knows how much I love him, how much it hurts. Why does he want to hurt me?'

'Oh come on, Anna.' I pluck the sleeve of the sweater she designed herself. She stares down at the black wool, fingering the fringing.

'OK OK, I know I've been ratty lately. I know it annoys your dad when there suddenly isn't any bloody butter. It annoys me too! But surely that's no reason to stay out all night?'

'It's not all night. He'll be back soon. And it's not because of the butter. Or you being ratty. It's your job. Don't you see, Anna? He can't stand it.'

'But he was quite supportive at first. He knew I was so bored just staying at home, especially after Eggs started school. He *encouraged* me—'

'Yeah, but that was when he thought it was just going to be some little sideline – Anna's new hobby to earn a bit of pin money. But now you've taken off, you've become really successful—'

'And I don't know how I'm going to cope. I need to expand, take on all sorts of staff. I need someone to look after Eggs when I'm tied up. I asked your dad if he'd pick him up from school more often. I mean, it's not often he's teaching late afternoon. But he practically blew his top and said he was a lecturer, not a child-minder.'

'See! It *is* what's getting to him.'

'But most men share childcare now.'

'Not old men like Dad! He's improved a bit. I mean, when I was little he didn't even put me to bed. I think he'd have passed out if he'd had to mop me up or feed me. My mum did it all.'

'Your mum did everything,' Anna sobs. 'She's the real true love of your dad's life, I know that. I know I can't ever replace her. I don't *want* to – but you've no idea how awful it is knowing that you're always going to come second best, with him, with you—'

'Oh, Anna. Mum was *different*. I'm sure Dad loves you just as much. And look at Eggs, he absolutely worships you. You're definitely first with him.'

'Not any more, not after I yelled at him this morning. I tried to make it up to him after school today but he acted so *warily*, as if I was about to explode any second. Then I had to see these three women who are going to knit up the bunny designs. I'd so much hoped your dad would be home to look after Eggs, but he didn't come and I was starting to get worried about him. One of these wretched women didn't seem skilled enough and I don't think she'll be able to cope. Another one's expecting a baby soon so maybe she won't be able to cope either. All the time I was trying to discuss things Eggs kept showing off and interrupting and driving me crazy so in the end I shouted at him. He ran away and hid. It took me ages to find him, under his bed, covered in dust. That's another thing – I never have time to do any proper housework. Poor little Eggs cried and said I was a mean mummy and he wanted his old mummy back—'

'Oh, Anna!' I can't help laughing.

She starts giggling weakly too, though the tears are still running down her cheeks. 'It's not really funny,' she says. 'Maybe . . . maybe I *should* give it all up, the knitwear design? That's really the whole answer, isn't it? It's not fair on Eggs. Maybe it's not fair on you or your dad either.'

'That's rubbish!' I take hold of Anna's shoulders and give her a little shake. 'Come on, Anna, don't be mad! It's wonderful that you've been so successful. You couldn't possibly give any of it up, not now.'

'I don't think I could bear it, I must admit. I know I'm tired all the time, and worried about getting everything done, but you've no idea how great it makes me feel, seeing the finished result, especially when it turns out just the way I wanted.'

'There! So you can't possibly let Dad stop you.'

'But the thing is, I *love* him. And you know and I know what he's up to right this minute, and I can't *stand* it.' Anna starts crying again.

'Look, let's go to bed, come on,' I say, helping her to her feet and leading her to the door.

'What am I going to do now? Lie all by myself on my side of the bed, staring up at the ceiling?' Anna weeps as we go up the stairs. 'And then what am I going to do when he eventually comes home? Pretend to be asleep? I've done that before, Ellie, just to keep the peace, but I don't think I can do it any more. It hurts too much.'

It's a relief when Eggs starts wailing sleepily, calling for Anna.

'Oh God,' Anna groans, but she straightens up, wipes her eyes and glides into his bedroom. 'What's up, little Eggs?' she murmurs softly. 'Is it your cold, my poppet? Let Mummy blow that poor old nose.'

Eggs snuffles something about a nasty man and Anna there-theres him and tells him there's no nasty man, it's all a silly old dream. I listen, feeling sick and shaky, wishing I was as young as Eggs and could be as easily reassured.

I hate being old enough to know what's really going on between Dad and Anna. I want to be told that they're very happy together, that my dad's not a nasty man and this is all a bad dream and soon we'll all wake up properly and Dad will be here, his arm round Anna, smiling and whistling and larking about, his old happy self.

Long after I go to my own bed I hear Dad come in and creep up the stairs. I wait, straining my ears. Then I hear the whispering start. My stomach turns over. I pull the sheets over my head and hunch up really small, trying to blot it all out.

I pretend Mum is still here for me. She's in bed with me, cuddling me close, telling me Myrtle Mouse stories. And then slowly, gradually, as I think about Myrtle, she starts to scamper about in my head, happy at first, her blue whiskers twitching, tail at a perky angle. She lives in a doll's house with

Mama Mouse and Papa Mouse. But Papa Mouse scampers off and doesn't come back and Mama Mouse has a new litter of baby mice and has no time for Myrtle — so she packs her spotty nightie and her whisker brush and her dormouse doll, makes herself a big cheese sandwich, and sets off into the big wide world . . .

I fall asleep and dream Myrtle Mouse stories. I wake up very early. I sit up and listen. The house is quiet. I can't hear Anna crying or Dad arguing. Eggs seems to be sound asleep. I twist my ring round and round my finger, wondering if it's all over now — or only just beginning.

Chapter Seven

Girls cry when

their friends
have secrets

Seven
Girls cry when their friends have secrets

I haven't done any of my homework but that can't be helped. I get out my sketchbook and spend an hour or more drafting little versions of Myrtle. It's fun designing different outfits for her. I decide she looks cutest in little dungarees with embroidered daisies and a matching daisy ear-stud in one round mouse ear. I experiment with her footwear. I try out dancing slippers and big boots and girly strappy sandals. I give her a little knapsack to pack when she leaves home.

Then I invent various adventures. I really put poor little Myrtle through a lot of trauma. It's like she's caught up in a little Mousy Melodrama. She's stalked by cats, chased by dogs, and attacked by a gang of rat-boys. She enjoys a gargantuan feast in a kitchen but very very nearly ends up in a mousetrap. She has a sore paw and is nursed back to health by a motherly hamster (Fudge resurrected). She goes on a long night trek with a gothic girl rat with twenty rings through her tail, and attends a muddy gig at Rodentbury.

I'm so soothed by my imaginary world of Myrtle that I almost forget the horrible Dad and Anna situation. I hear Anna get up, I hear her in the bathroom, I hear her chivvy Eggs into getting washed and dressed, but it's impossible to tell from her tone how she is.

Maybe it's all right again. Maybe Dad has a perfectly reasonable excuse for why he stayed out half the night. Maybe Dad and Anna made it all up after their argument. Maybe they'll be all over each other at breakfast, the way they used to be.

I always hated it when Dad wound his arm round Anna's waist and she nestled up to him. I'd give anything to see them snuggled up together now. But when I go down to the kitchen there's no arm-winding, no nestling. Anna is talking softly to Eggs, babying him with his cereal, letting him sit on her lap while he eats it. Dad is standing at the sink, drinking a mug of coffee, not looking at anyone, not speaking, acting like he doesn't belong to our family any more.

I look at Anna's sore eyes and white face. I feel so angry with Dad. How *dare* he mess around with her, mess around with all our lives?

'Dad? Dad, can I have a word with you?' I say, going up to him.

'What? Look, Ellie, I'm in a bit of a rush. Can't it wait?' says Dad, putting his coffee cup down and making for the door.

'No, it can't wait, Dad,' I say fiercely. 'I want to know what's going on. Where were you last night?'

'Don't, Ellie, not now,' Anna says quickly.

'Why not? Why can't I ask? What are you playing at, Dad? Why are you doing this?' I stand in front of him, chin up, fists clenched.

Dad looks angry too, his eyes blazing. 'Just mind your own business, Ellie,' he says, pushing past me. 'This has got nothing to do with you.'

'It's got everything to do with me!' I shout.

'Not in front of Eggs,' Anna pleads as Dad walks out.

'But it's to do with him too, with all of us.' I run after Dad into the hall. 'You've got no right to mess around with us like this, Dad. Can't you see how unhappy you're making Anna? Just because you're jealous of her!'

'So you think I'm jealous?' says Dad, opening the front door.

'Yes, because Anna's doing so well. You can't stand it. That's just so typical of the whole male ego. You can't bear to be overshadowed. You didn't let my mother work, did you, even though she was brilliant at Art.'

'You know nothing about it,' says Dad. 'Your mother didn't want to work. She wanted to look after you.'

'Yes, but I bet she'd have wanted to work once I was at school. She'd have been a brilliant graphic artist, just like Anna's brilliant at her designing. That's what you can't stick, Dad. You're not brilliant. You want us all to look up to you and think you're wonderful. Well, you're not. The only thing you're brilliant at is making us all unhappy.'

'Well, now I know,' says Dad, and he walks out, slamming the door.

I'm left standing there, wondering if I want to go shrieking down the front path after him.

Maybe I've said enough.

I'm shaking. Anna comes and puts her arm round me, taking me back into the kitchen. She pours me a cup of tea. Eggs is staring at us, his spoon of cereal dripping slowly up his sweater sleeve.

'You shouted at Dad, Ellie!' says Eggs. 'You'll get into *big* trouble.'

'I don't care,' I say, sipping my tea. My teeth clink against the china. I look at Anna. 'I'm sorry. I just couldn't help coming out with it.'

'I know,' says Anna, patting my shoulder. 'Don't worry so, Ellie. It might just all blow over.'

'It might not,' I say and I give her a quick hug.

I think about what might happen as I walk to the bus stop. I play the kids' game of not stepping on the cracks of the pavement. If I can make it all the way to school then Dad and Anna won't split up. I used to long for that to happen. I wanted Anna to clear off with Eggs so that it could be just Dad and me. But now that's not what I want at all. I'd hate it to be just Dad and me – or Dad and me and some new girlfriend. I'd feel as out of it as Russell.

I think of him longingly. I touch my ring, twisting it round and round. Maybe we'll stay together for ever and then we'll have our own place. We won't ever be lonely any more. We'll have each other . . .

I close my eyes and whisper Russell's name – and very nearly walk straight into the blond guy, Mr Dream Man. He sidesteps neatly.

'Whoops! Collision avoided – just!'

'I've got my punchbag rucksack under control, don't worry.'

'Not in such a hurry today? What were you day-dreaming about, eh? Your boyfriend?'

'Maybe,' I say, blushing.

'Ah, sweet! True love, eh?'

'I think so.'

I *know* so. I think about Russell all the way to school. I remember the way he kissed me just last night. I feel my whole body weaken at the thought of his touch. But at the corner of my mind's eye little Ellie Elephant droops her head, trunk trailing, forced to do all sorts of new tricks for Russell when she's mine and she only wants to do things *my* way.

I can't wait to see Magda and Nadine. I desperately need to tell them all about Dad and Anna and see if they think this is deadly serious.

I *also* want to ask them about Russell and exactly how far they think I should go. We often talk about it. We even have different numbers for various activities. Nadine went *way* down the list with Liam, but Magda has always been surprisingly prim and insists she's never going to do more than kiss until she's in a proper relationship later on. But this is now, not later, and Russell and I are in a proper relationship. I need Magda and Nadine's *advice*.

They're both at school when I get there, sitting

squashed up together on a desk, legs dangling. Nadine whispers to Magda and they both splutter with laughter.

'Hi! What's the big joke, then?' I say.

They look at each other. Nadine shakes her head ever so slightly. 'Oh, nothing,' she says.

'Yeah, we were just messing about,' says Magda.

I stare at them, my heart thudding. Nothing! They've got some private secret joke going between them and I'm not in on it. But we always share everything. We're best friends, the three of us. I suddenly feel like some sad little toddler shut out of the Wendy house at nursery school while my two little friends play happily inside.

'Come on, you guys. It's *me*, Ellie.' Then I get it. 'Oh, so the joke was about me, right?'

'Wrong,' says Magda, but she isn't looking me in the eye.

'Mags? Naddie? Look, you were laughing your heads off and then you looked up and saw me and shut up quick. So you were obviously having a laugh about me.'

'Oh Ellie, don't be so paranoid,' says Nadine, sliding down from the desk and reaching in her schoolbag for her hairbrush. 'We were having a little joke about a *boy*, if you must know.'

'Yeah, but which boy? My Russell, by any chance?' I say, starting to get angry now.

'Oooh, *your* Russell, eh?' says Nadine. 'You're such a couple now, Ellie. Yet you were always the one who nagged me for abandoning my girlfriends when I went out with Liam.'

'You got all shirty with me too when I went out

with Mick, remember? Yet now you don't even dream of coming round to my place to help me get over poor Fudge's death. You just rush off with Russell.'

I blink at them both. What's the matter with them? We're not quarrelling, are we? I can't stand it if we are. They're my best friends. Nadine and Magda mean all the world to me.

I didn't realize they'd be so upset because I didn't go round to Magda's for their little-girly pet funeral. And I'm not sure Magda's *that* devastated about her hamster. She never made a fuss of Fudge when she was alive. Still, I do feel a little bit bad that I didn't go round to her place.

'Did you have a proper funeral?' I ask humbly.

'We certainly did,' says Nadine.

'Yeah, Naddie made the most brilliant coffin. She painted a shoe box black and lined it with a purple silk scarf. I popped poor little Fudge into this black lace glove. She looked *so* sweet, though she'd started to get just a little bit stinky. Oh dear!' Magda sniffs mournfully.

I'm starting to wish I'd gone after all.

'We had this amazing gothic funeral. Well, more Viking, really, because we ended up sending Fudge off on a little sail towards Hamster Valhalla.'

'We were going to dig a grave but Magda just had this ancient plastic seaside spade and I mucked up two of my nails scrabbling in all that earth, so we took Fudge down to the river instead.'

'In a procession, both of us wearing black veils. These boys biked past us and started yelling stuff, so I said we were going to a funeral and they should

73

show more respect. Then they felt really mean and started chatting properly, but Nadine sent them packing.'

'Well, they were just kids.'

'They were Year Ten!'

'Yeah, like I said. *Kids*,' says Nadine.

'Just because you're seeing this nineteen-year-old,' I say.

Nadine looks at Magda. Magda looks back. They give each other a secret little smirk.

'*What?*' I say. 'Oh come on, don't be like that. Magda. Nad. *Tell* me!'

But Mrs Henderson comes trotting into class in her trainers and tells us all to be quiet.

I'll have to find out later.

Chapter Eight

Eight
Girls cry when their friends say they're fat

I have to wait until lunchtime. There's no time at all at break. Mrs Henderson keeps us so late at PE that we're still on the flipping hockey pitch when the bell goes. We waste a full fifteen minutes rushing in and out of the showers and shoving our clothes back on. I ladder my tights trying to yank them up too quickly. My hair goes horribly frizzy and *won't* get brushed into submission. I feel like throwing my hairbrush at the mirror.

I *hate* the way I look. Magda and Nadine have got such gorgeous figures. Nadine looks so slender and willowy and wonderful. Magda is very curvy but in all the right places. I curve *everywhere*. I just hate my stomach bulging over my knickers and my whacking great thighs, especially when they're bright pink from running round the hockey pitch.

Maybe I'll try to lose just a little bit of weight again. I won't go really mad like last term. But if I just lost a few pounds . . .

It's pizza for lunch. I'm so starving hungry I eat a huge slice, *and* chips. Then I decide I might as well go the whole hog now, and select a big cream bun for pudding.

Magda, Nadine and I go to our favourite nattering nook on the steps by the Portakabins. We squash up together on the same step, me in the middle. Thank goodness we seem to be friends again.

'We *are* friends, aren't we?' I say pathetically, putting my arms round both of them.

'Of course we're friends, nutcase,' says Nadine.

'You are daft, Ellie. We're friends for ever, you know that,' says Magda.

'So why have you got this secret between the two of you, eh?' I say, giving them a little shake. 'Come on, tell me, or I'll knock your heads together.'

'Go on, Naddie, tell her,' says Magda.

'Well . . . Ellie, do you promise you won't go all po-faced and naggle at me?' says Nadine.

'Of course I won't! Why? What have you done?'

'I haven't done *anything*,' says Nadine. 'It's just . . . well, you know I mentioned this guy Ellis—'

'Ah! So what have you done with *him*?'

'Nothing. Truly. We haven't so much as shaken hands,' says Nadine.

Magda bursts out laughing. 'He hasn't half confided in you, though, Naddie,' she says.

'Shut *up*, Mags,' says Nadine.

That's it. They're doing it again. Keeping me

right out of things. I can't stand it. I take my arms off their shoulders and struggle to stand up.

'Ellie?'

'Where are you going?'

'I know when I'm not wanted,' I mumble.

'Oh, for heaven's *sake*, Ellie!'

'Sit *down*, girl!'

Nadine pulls on my arm and Magda tackles me round the knees so that I collapse in a heap on top of them. We roll around, groaning and then giggling. It's hopeless trying to stay huffy when you're sandwiched between two giggly girls and all your arms and legs are mixed up together.

When we eventually get straightened out Magda blurts out, 'Nadine met her Ellis guy on the Internet!'

'Mags! You swore you wouldn't tell,' says Nadine.

'Why didn't you tell me before? The Internet! Oh, Naddie, are you *crackers*?'

'There! I *know* it! That's precisely why I didn't want you to know. Your face, Ellie! You look so shocked.'

'Well, no wonder. You're not saying you met him in one of those chatrooms? You didn't!'

'She *did*,' says Magda.

'I did *not*. We met up on this *Xanadu* website, right – you know, Ellie, I told you. It's this truly gothic cool comic book—'

'Oh yeah, yeah, I like those graphics, especially the way they have the picture boxes all different sizes and the characters step right out of the black lines—'

'Oh God, don't go all technical on us. Save the Art talk for Russell,' says Nadine. 'I just like *Xanadu* because it's a great scary story with this fantastic girl heroine with long black hair and very white skin – a bit like me, actually!'

'Except you don't walk around in a black micro bikini and black boots up to your thighs,' says Magda, giggling. 'Anyway, Ellie, Nadine's got chatting to this guy on the *Xanadu* website and now they're e-mailing each other every night. I joined in too last night after poor Fudge's funeral. Ellis is so *cool*. Well, he's a bit cheeky, actually – some of the things he was asking Nadine were pretty blatant, but I suppose that's guys for you—'

'What sort of things?'

So Magda tells me.

'*Nadine!* You didn't reply, did you?'

'Look, Mags, I wish you'd kept your mouth shut. Ellie's getting to sound like my mother,' says Nadine, rolling her eyes.

'You haven't told your mother, have you?'

Nadine's eyes practically disappear. 'Are you nuts? Of course not! She'd go crackers.'

'You *are* crackers, Nad! Why won't you ever get involved with anyone *normal*?'

'Normal is *boring*. I'm not like you two. I don't want silly boys like Russell and Greg.'

'Russell *isn't* silly,' I protest.

'Greg is,' says Magda. 'He might have learned how to kiss but he's still useless at conversation – whereas Ellis says the most *amazing* things.'

'I'll bet!'

'No, lovely romantic things, Ellie. He really *communicates* with Nadine. His messages are just like poetry.'

'When I logged on this morning he said he's actually writing a poem about me,' Nadine says proudly. 'He's calling it "My Xanadu Girl".'

'What are you *playing* at, Nadine? He'll be fantasizing that *you're* wearing a black bikini and thigh-high boots, like some pervy creep.'

'Don't you dare call him a pervy creep!' says Nadine, blushing. 'And so what if he does? It's just harmless fantasy.'

'I'd die if I thought some bloke was getting off on the thought of me like that,' I say.

'Yeah, well, it's not very likely, is it, Ellie? I mean, you're so fat you'd look plain ridiculous in a bikini and big boots,' says Nadine.

Magda gasps. There's a little silence. I can't believe she's said it. OK, it's *true* – but it's so hateful of her. I feel the tears stinging my eyes. I stand up shakily.

'Oh, sit back down, Ellie, please,' says Magda. 'Don't go all huffy again.'

'You heard what she said!'

'Yeah, but she didn't mean it.'

'She called Ellis a pervy creep!' says Nadine.

'She didn't mean that either!' says Magda.

Nadine and I look at each other. We *did* mean it. This isn't just a silly squabble, over in five minutes. This is a serious argument. This is us almost breaking friends. In fact there's no almost about it.

'Bye,' I say, marching off, holding my head high. So high that I trip going up the steps and give my shin a crack. It hurts a lot. Maybe that's why the tears are pouring down my cheeks.

Chapter Nine

Girls cry when

they quarrel with their friends

Nine
Girls cry when they quarrel with their friends

I sniff fiercely, not wanting to wipe my eyes while Nadine and Magda can still see me.

Nadine and Magda. There's no sound of footsteps behind me, no arm round my waist, no word in my ear. Magda's chosen to stay with Nadine. *They're* the best friends now. Yet Nadine's always been *my* friend, back since we were in nursery school together. When we went to Anderson's I was the one who made friends with Magda. Nadine didn't like her much for ages. I always had to negotiate between them, piggy-in-the-middle.

Now I'm just Piggy.

Fat Piggy.

I can't bear it. How can she be so mean? She *knows* how self-conscious I am about the way I look. She knows I was almost anorexic last term. Does she want me to regress right back and start dieting obsessively all over again?

I'm not going to let her get to me. I'm not going to take it to heart.

But as I sit stiffly by myself all afternoon at school I feel as if Nadine has written FAT in big block capitals all over my back. It hurts so. Literally. I have to keep rubbing it. And my stomach starts hurting too. It's bigger than ever, a hateful huge watermelon stretching my skirt. I pummel it under my desk. The pain is getting worse. It's grimly familiar now, that sick squeezing feeling. I'm starting my period.

I need to charge home the second the bell goes for the end of school. I hesitate just for a moment, wondering whether Nadine might look in my direction. She's been studiedly ignoring me ever since lunch, even though we sit so near each other. But she's calmly packing her bag, chatting to Magda. Magda glances round at me, looking anxious. She smiles at me – but she stays by Nadine's side.

Well, I'm not going to hang around hoping they'll make friends with me. I can't, anyway. I need to get to the bathroom at home to sort myself out. I give the back of my skirt one quick check and rush off.

'Ellie? Wait!' Magda calls. And then she adds, 'Don't be so childish!'

How dare she! I'm not being childish in the slightest. I'm the one acting like a responsible grown-up. Nadine is the silly idiot, letting a total stranger send her stupid messages. He could be *anyone*. Ellis sounds a deeply suspect name for a start. Maybe he really *is* a creepy pervert.

I'm furious with Nadine, but of course I still love her to bits underneath. I don't want her to get into serious trouble. She's made it plain she won't listen to me. So maybe I should tell someone? Nadine's mum or dad? No, I *can't*. Nadine would kill me. She and Magda would never talk to me ever again.

'Ellie! Hey, Ellie!'

Oh God, it's Russell standing by the school gate. I very nearly walk straight past him. 'Oh, Russell, sorry!'

'You were deep in thought! Thinking about me, eh?'

'Well, I was actually worrying about Nadine because—'

'Because you're obsessed with her and Magda – I know,' says Russell irritably. 'I don't know why you bother seeing me sometimes. You'd be far happier going round in your girly threesome all the time.'

'We've had a row, if you must know,' I say. 'Listen, I'm very worried about Nadine, she's gone completely crazy and—'

'She *is* crazy. Look, forget her, forget Magda. Come back to my place and we'll have a lovely time, just the two of us.'

'I can't.'

'Why not?'

I *can't* tell him that I need to be in my own bathroom as soon as possible. I know you should be able to talk to your boyfriend about anything. We *do* talk about some stuff. But not that. I'd feel so embarrassed.

'I – I don't feel very well,' I say, truthfully enough. 'I just want to go home and lie down.'

'Come and lie down with me instead,' says Russell.

'Oh sure,' I say.

'I'll be sweet to you. I'll massage your forehead – and your shoulders – and anywhere else we can think of . . .'

'Leave it out!' I wish he wouldn't be quite so insistent all the time. I love it that he cares about me and loves me, but just recently all he seems to want to do is see how far he can go with me. I love the things we do together but sometimes I wish he'd relate more to me as Ellie the *person*, not Ellie the body.

My body is letting me down big time. My stomach squeezes. I feel an alarming dampness. 'I'm sorry, Russell, I really have to go home *now*,' I say, and I start running.

I'm in a right state when I eventually make it home. Anna's left a note to say she's gone up to town to see the buyer of a big chain store who's interested in some special bargain children's knitwear, designed by Anna but produced on a massive scale.

'It'll mean heaps more work if it comes off, so I'm not sure I'll say yes,' Anna's scribbled to me. 'You know what the Dad situation is like.'

'Definitely say yes, Anna,' I mutter. 'Never you mind Dad.'

I read on. Oh God. Eggs has gone to tea with Natasha, Nadine's little sister.

'I hope to be back around sixish, but if I'm

delayed can you be an angel and go and collect Eggs, Ellie?' Anna writes.

Let's hope she's *not* delayed. I don't want to go anywhere near Nadine's, not now.

It's lovely to have the house to myself just for once. I have a long hot bath, lying back under the bubbles and stroking my poor sore swollen tummy.

FAT.

No! I'm not going to think about Nadine. Or Magda. Or Dad. Or Anna and Eggs. Or even Russell. I'm going to think about me.

I towel myself dry, put on my comfy old dungarees and a stripy sweatshirt and then sit cross-legged on my bed drawing Myrtle Mouse. She has any number of scary adventures. She even runs away to London and becomes an Underground mouse, lurking in tunnels and diving for cover every time the terrifying tube roars past. Her beautiful blue fur turns sooty black and she loses the tip of her tail when she only just manages to scamper clear of a maintenance man's big boot.

I make sure she has a happy ending, though. A little girl bribes her up onto the platform with a cheese sandwich, wraps her grimy little body in a tissue and then pops her in her pocket. Myrtle is taken home and tenderly cleaned up and cared for and given a splendid new home. It's another doll's house, but this time it's her very own Myrtle Mansions, with colour-co-ordinated blue willow-pattern wallpaper in the kitchen and blue roses in the living room and midnight blue with tiny silver stars in the bedroom.

When I finish I gently stroke little Myrtle's

crayon head as she snuggles under her dark blue duvet in the very last picture. Then I find a big envelope and address it. I write a note explaining that I don't have a competition form and I know I'm a bit late entering anyway, but can they please have a look at the enclosed all the same.

Anna isn't back by six. There's no sign of Dad either. So I have to be the responsible big sister.

I post my Myrtle drawings on my way round to Nadine's. I feel stupidly nervous as I walk up the neat gravel path to her front door. My footsteps go crunch crunch crunch. My stomach goes clench clench clench.

Nadine's mum answers the door, looking a little distracted. There are shrieks of laughter coming from the kitchen – very youthful high-pitched laughter.

'Oh, it's you, Eleanor. Come in, dear. I was expecting your mother.'

'Yes, sorry, she's tied up with some work thing.'

'Well, I do hope you've come to collect your brother, dear. He's getting a little over-excited. Not really a good idea so near bedtime. He tipped his orange juice all down himself so I had to change his clothes. I was going to dress him in Natasha's jeans and a jersey but I'm afraid he had other ideas.'

Right on cue Eggs dashes out of the kitchen, chased by Natasha. *She* is wearing her jeans, with her long hair crammed under a baseball cap. She's wearing Eggs' clompy boys' shoes. Oh God. Eggs is wearing Natasha's flounciest pink party frock. He's got various pink slides stuck in his short hair, bangles up and down his arms, and he's shuffling in high heels with diamanté bows.

'Hi, Ellie-Belly! I'm your sister Eggerina, and this is my boyfriend Nat,' Eggs squeaks in a silly falsetto voice.

My brother, mini transvestite.

'Get that dress off this minute, Eggs. You'll muck it up,' I say. 'Come on, we've got to go home.'

Eggs takes no notice whatsoever. He barges past with a joyous whoop and starts doing a can-can, staggering in his high heels. Natasha shrieks with laughter as he shows all of us he's even appropriated her frilly knickers.

'Leave him to me,' says Nadine's mother wearily. 'You go and talk to Nadine. She's in the study working on the computer. She's finding the Internet so useful for her homework nowadays.'

I'll bet. I don't want to go and see her but neither do I want to let her mum know we're not speaking. I shuffle towards the study. Nadine is crouched in front of the computer screen, smirking at some e-mail message. She jumps in alarm when I come into the room, quickly closing down everything on the screen – and then she sees it's just me. We look at each other. We both go pink.

'Ellie?'

'Nadine?'

There's a little pause. What's the matter with us? We're best friends, always have been, always will be.

'It's your little fat friend,' I say shakily.

'Oh El, I'm sorry.'

'I'm sorry too,' I say.

We both rush at each other and hug.

'We are such nuts,' I say.

'I know, I know. Ellie, I didn't *mean* it.'

'And I didn't mean to come on all pious and po-faced about — you know . . .' I wave at the blank computer screen.

'I know it's a bit risky. I know you do get some nuts on line. But Ellis is so different, Ellie. He's just . . . oh, like the guy of my dreams. He says such amazing things. And he wants to know all about me. He doesn't go on and on about himself the way Liam did. He doesn't try to kid me he's Mr Cool. He confides all sorts of stuff about himself, how he's shy and scared of all kinds of things. He says if we ever met he'd probably be struck dumb and unable to think of a thing to say.'

'You're not *going* to meet him, are you?' I ask, alarm bells ringing.

'No, no, of course not,' Nadine says quickly. 'Don't look so worried, Ellie, He's lovely, he really is. Look, I'll show you.'

She switches her computer back on and finds me some of his early messages. And he does sound lovely. He chats for ages about *Xanadu* and what fantasy means to him and how he's read *The Lord of the Rings* five whole times but it's such a *boy* book, and how *Xanadu* is great because it's all about girls and he loves girls. He goes on about how he'd always had this dream girl in his head from when he was about twelve, a strange, shy gothic girl he could share everything with. He doesn't want to be forward or rush things but he feels Nadine is this girl, only better, because she's so beautiful, much prettier than the actress who plays Xanadu in the TV series . . .

'Then he goes into some really personal stuff. I'm not showing you, Ellie. I haven't even shown Magda some of it.'

'Oh come *on*, Nad, please!'

So she shows me. I read it, my heart thumping. There's a part of me that still thinks this is crazy. There's a complete stranger writing all sorts of intimate things to Nadine when she's only fourteen, for God's sake. But he *does* write beautifully. It's not sleazy at all, it's tender and exciting and romantic. It's the sort of thing I wish wish wish Russell would say to me.

Chapter Ten

Girls cry when their boyfriends don't understand

Ten
Girls cry when their boyfriends don't understand

'Oh, Ellie, I love you.'

Kisses.

'Oh, Ellie, I love you.'

More kisses.

'Oh, Ellie, I love you. Please.'

More than kisses.

'Oh, Ellie, I love you. Please, please, please.'

Struggles. Sulks. Another kiss. Sometimes it's a kiss goodnight. Sometimes we start the whole routine all over again. It's starting to get a bit . . . boring.

No it's not! What's the matter with me? I *love* Russell. He's the only boy in the world for me. I wear his ring all the time. It's just that we've got into this same little routine every time we see each other. Russell always always always says the same things.

I can't help wishing he'd be as inventive as Nadine's Ellis. I make up an entire alternative scenario in my head, with Russell saying and indeed doing the most delightful and unexpected things. Our own undignified little snogging sessions seem so pathetic by comparison. No, not *pathetic*. There I go again, picking holes, being so fussy. It's not as if *I'm* all that great at being romantic and making things wonderful for Russell. There's one thing he keeps begging me to do and I *nearly* do it, but then I can't help getting a fit of the giggles. Russell gets really annoyed with me, which only makes me splutter more.

'Do you always have to be so giggly, Ellie?' he asks, exasperated.

'Well, I'm a girl. All girls giggle. It goes with the territory.'

'Yeah, but some girls know when it's appropriate to be a bit *serious*,' says Russell.

'Then why don't you go off with some of these girls then?' I say, starting to get in a huff.

'You know you're the only girl in the whole world for me,' Russell says.

I calm down and kiss him lovingly. He can still be so sweet a lot of the time. It's just that I wish he wasn't *always* trying to push me into doing stuff I don't want to. Well, sometimes I want to do it as much as him, of course I do, but I don't somehow feel *ready* for that kind of relationship.

'Jeff's girlfriend Julie lets him. And Jamie and Big Mac have done it with heaps of girls.'

'So they say,' I sigh irritably. 'Do you discuss *our* love life with all your mates in Year Eleven?'

'No!' says Russell, though he's gone a little pink. 'Anyway, I know for a fact you tell Magda and Nadine everything so don't be such a hypocrite.'

'I don't tell them. Well, not much,' I say. 'Nowhere near as much as they tell me. You should hear some of the things Nadine's Ellis says to her!'

'What about Magda? Who's she seeing at the moment?'

'Well, no one really. She was wondering whether to get back with Greg, but now she thinks he's insensitive. Her hamster had this terribly traumatic terminal accident and Greg wanted to give her little new baby hamsters Toffee and Mallow straight away, but Magda says she's still mourning and she can't bear to get involved with any other hamsters at the moment. She doesn't really want to get involved with Greg *either*.'

'Oh great,' says Russell. 'Because Big Mac's having a big do for his birthday and most of the guys in my class are coming, right, but there's a distinct shortage of girls.'

'Magda's not *that* sort of girl,' I say fiercely. 'I know what your mate Big Mac is like.'

'No no, this is a proper party, dead respectable, parents in the background, I swear. I promised Big Mac we'd go. That's OK, isn't it?'

'Well, you could have asked first. You never tell me things, Russell. Like that Art competition—'

'Don't nag, Ellie! OK, OK, point taken. I'm sorry, I should have told you sooner. Still, there'll be heaps more competitions.'

'But you're not to appropriate my Ellie Elephant ever again,' I say, tapping him on the nose.

'She's not *your* elephant. Anyone can draw a flipping elephant.'

'Not a cute girl one with a twisty trunk and painted toenails. She's Ellie Elephant. My invention.' I tap a little harder.

'Ouch! Stop it, missy,' says Russell, grabbing me by the wrists.

We play at wrestling, mucking about at first – but then Russell starts to get serious again.

'Oh, Ellie, I love you. Please.'

'Russell! You've got a one-track mind.'

'Look, if I win the competition I'll share the prize with you, seeing as you insist you invented the silly little elephant.'

This is sweet and generous of him. Though I still find it annoying. And I don't want this wrestling match to develop.

'Stop it, Russell. I've got to go now. I've got to get to the shops before they shut.'

'You'd sooner go boring old shopping than be with me?' Russell says, sounding peeved.

'I'm not shopping for me. It's food shopping for all the family.'

I told Anna at breakfast I'd go to Waitrose for her as she was tied up with so much work. I said it pointedly in front of Dad. I knew it would get to him.

'Look, we'll all go on Sunday,' Dad said. 'Stop looking at me like that, Ellie. You don't have to play the martyr.'

It wouldn't work if we all went shopping on Sunday as a family. We're not *acting* like a family now. Dad and Anna are barely speaking. Dad stays out late most evenings. Anna works solidly. She has a permanent little worry frown on her forehead and dark circles under her eyes. Eggs is forever whining, even though Anna keeps buying him little treats to keep him happy. He's started to cling to Anna like a baby. I know Anna's really worried about him. I don't want her to have to worry about me too.

I do all the shopping, even though it's more boring and bothersome than I thought. I can't find half the stuff. I have to trail round every single aisle. I stand in the check-out queue for ages. There's just one woman in front of me now. I start getting all the stuff out the trolley and then sneeze. I fumble in my pocket for a tissue. Oh no. *Tissues*. I forgot all about them.

I charge back for them, my trolley careering wildly on its wobbly wheels, and bash right into this tall blond guy in a white hat and overall filling up the fridge with cartons of milk. He drops a carton and we both hold our breath – but it doesn't split or spill.

'So we don't have to cry over spilt milk,' I say, wondering why he's grinning at me in such a familiar way. And then I realize. He's not just *any* tall blond guy. He's my Mr Dream Man, the boy I bump into on the way to school. Literally. And now I've done it again. 'I'm so *sorry*! Honestly, I don't always bash into people.'

'Only when I'm around!'

'I didn't realize you worked here.'

'Well, I can't really feel like Joe Cool in this gear,' he says, tipping his funny hygiene hat into a rakish angle. 'But it's an OK job just for now. I'm having a gap year before starting at university.'

'I'm definitely going to have a gap year too,' I say. 'My girlfriends and I have got it all worked out. Six months' work and then six months' travelling . . .'

I want to go somewhere wonderful like Australia. Nadine fancies somewhere more exotic like India. Magda wants to hire a car and drive all over America – well, if she's passed her driving test.

I tell him all this and he listens politely, but you can tell he's really thinking, Yeah, well, *maybe*. He tells me about his month Euro-railing, staying on campsites. I don't think much of camping. We always used to go camping in Wales before we got the cottage. It was so damp and so dreary and ants got in my sleeping bag and I'm pretty certain a mouse ran over my face in the night. It *could* just have been my own hair but I screamed my head off anyway.

I'm telling Mr Dream Man all about it and he's laughing. Then I look up and there's *Russell* standing staring at us, even though we said goodbye half an hour ago.

'Russell! What are you doing here?'

'Don't worry. Don't let me interrupt,' he says in a surly tone.

'I'd better get back to work anyway,' Mr Dream Man says quickly. He leans his head close to me. 'Is he the boyfriend? He's *nice*.'

Russell isn't acting a *bit* nice. He's marching off so quickly I have to gallop after him, my trolley veering wildly left and right so that little old ladies and mums with toddlers have to leap for their lives.

'Russell, wait, will you!' I bellow in frustration. 'What are you doing here?'

'I felt mean leaving you to do all this shopping. I thought the least I could do was come and find you and help you carry it. I had no idea *why* you suddenly had this urgent desire to act like the Wonder Woman of Waitrose.'

'What?' I blink at him.

'Don't come the wide-eyed innocent with me, Ellie! I had no idea you had a thing going with that shelf-stacker guy in the silly hat.'

I burst out laughing, which makes Russell even more furious. 'Oh, Russell, listen. I hardly know him.'

'Oh yeah? The way he was looking at you made me feel sick. He obviously fancies you like mad.'

'The one thing I *do* know about him is he's gay.'

Now it's Russell's turn to stand with his mouth open. 'What?'

'He's gay, Russell. And if he fancies anyone, it's you. He said he thought you looked very *nice*. He's obviously smitten.'

Russell is going very pink. 'Right. Well. That's cool. Though I hope you made it plain you're my girlfriend.'

'You were acting like you're really jealous,' I say.

'Nah, of course I wasn't. I just thought you were making a monkey out of me.'

'But I wasn't.'

'That's right.'

'So we're still friends?'

'We're more than friends, silly,' says Russell, and he takes my hand and twists the ring lovingly on my finger.

He helps me carry the shopping all the way home. Anna is very grateful to us both. Russell's having a cup of tea with us when Dad comes home, early for the first time in ages. He's carrying a huge box of Sainsbury's groceries.

'Dad! *I* went to Waitrose,' I say.

'Well, we won't run short of butter and tissues for a while now,' says Dad.

'Thank you for getting all the stuff, anyway,' says Anna, fumbling in her handbag. 'How much did it come to? I'll pay you out of the housekeeping purse.'

'For God's sake, I can buy a few groceries. I can still earn a bob or two. Not as much as you, perhaps, but enough,' Dad says sharply.

It's hopeless. I thought they might just make it up now but they seem to be back to hating each other, though they have to be icily polite in front of Russell. I help Anna unpack the second lot of stuff, opening up Dad's box of tissues when I sneeze again. I do hope I'm not going down with Eggs' cold. He is over the sniffles and now coughs all over everywhere instead.

Dad and Russell make slightly uneasy small talk – uneasier still when Russell starts on about Cynthia rushing out to buy an Anna Allard designer sweater. Dad's conversation dwindles to the odd grunt. Russell realizes he's on quicksand and hauls himself to safety by talking about the Art competition. He has the nerve to boast about his elephant cartoons.

'*My* elephant,' I mutter.

Russell sighs. 'I told you, Ellie, if I win I'll go

fifty–fifty with you. Though it's not *your* elephant, it's *my* cartoon elephant.'

'Still, Ellie's always drawn dinky elephants ever since she was a little girl,' says Dad, drinking the cup of tea that Anna's poured for him, though he doesn't actually acknowledge her. 'Why didn't you do your elephant yourself, Ellie?'

'Oh, she was too late to enter the competition,' says Russell, as if I had simply been too idle to get it together in time.

'No, I did have a go,' I say. 'I didn't draw elephants, though. I did a little blue mouse.'

Dad looks up at me. 'Not *Myrtle* Mouse?'

'Yes.'

'Is this another of your special characters?' Russell asks. 'Can't I draw mice any more without you making a fuss? Maybe you'll tell the Walt Disney organization to watch out too!'

I ignore Russell. I'm looking at Dad. I rather hope he keeps quiet. He doesn't.

'Myrtle was invented by Ellie's mum,' says Dad.

Russell looks at Anna.

'No, her *real* mum.'

Anna flinches. I don't think Dad means it nastily. His whole face has softened.

'She made up Myrtle Mouse when Ellie was little. She wouldn't go to sleep until her mum made up a Myrtle Mouse story.'

'We made her up together, Dad. And I always drew pictures of her. Well, I used to copy Mum's at first, but then I did my own.'

'So you've copied your mum's drawings for the competition!' Russell shouts. 'You little hypocrite!

All that fuss about my copying Ellie Elephant. And I *didn't* copy you anyway.'

'I didn't copy my mum.'

'You just admitted it in front of all of us!' Russell insists.

'That was when I was *little*. I reinvented Myrtle. She's not a bit like the little mouse my mum made up, not now. She's mine,' I say defensively.

'Rubbish! If you've used your mum's design that's really cheating,' says Dad.

I want to kick him. Anna looks like she does too. 'Don't be so unfair! Ellie's just used a little child's character as a jumping-off point for her own art-work,' she says. 'Of course she's not cheating. What a thing to say to your own daughter! What's the matter with you?'

'I'm jealous, aren't I? At least, that's what my precious daughter thinks.'

'Dad! Anyway, I'm not even eligible for the stupid competition. I sent my entry in too late. They'll probably just chuck it in the bin.'

Chapter Eleven

Girls cry when

their dreams come true!

Eleven
Girls cry when their dreams come true!

I am dying. I'm hot all over and yet I'm shivering. My nose is all bunged up, my throat is raw, my head aches, my chest hurts. I know I'm really really ill. I'm sure I've got pneumonia. Double pneumonia. No, *triple*. Hang on, I've only got two lungs. It feels like they're both blown up like balloons, about to burst.

Everyone thinks I've just got Eggs' cold. This isn't a *cold*. How could anyone feel so awful with a mere cold? Yet no one seems remotely sympathetic. Dad and Anna made me go into school yesterday, which was so unfair. And a waste of time. I couldn't concentrate on any of the lessons and could barely crawl across the hockey pitch. OK OK, I suppose I'm *usually* inattentive and appalling at Games, but I couldn't even paint properly in Art, my best subject.

We are still stuck in the still-life slot. I like *animated* life a lot more, though I suppose Mr Windsor did his best to make it interesting for us. He showed us copies of these weirdly lovely seventeenth-century Spanish paintings of cabbages on string, and then he dangled a whole load of real cabbages in the air for us to copy. Magda had a little go at flicking one cabbage into another to see if they'd go *dong dong dong* backwards and forwards like those smart executive toys, but they just made a dull *thwack* and got their strings all tangled. Mr Windsor said if we didn't settle down sharpish he'd lop off our heads and string them up instead.

So we settled, sort of, though Magda kept moaning that the smell of cabbages was making her feel sick. I couldn't smell anything at all but I felt sick anyway. I tried hard at first but my cabbages looked like giant green roses and I lost heart. I painted in a little cartoon bunny up on its back legs, mouth open and drooling, desperately trying to leap up and reach the dangling feast. Magda and Nadine were duly appreciative but Mr Windsor wasn't amused.

'We all know you're an inventive cartoonist, Ellie, but it's getting a little bit predictable the way you fall back on cartoons whenever you're having trouble with a serious subject.'

'Oooh!' Magda said mockingly.

'That's enough, Magda! You three girls are starting to annoy me. I shall split the three of you up if you carry on like this.'

'No one could *ever* split us up,' Magda muttered, but not quite loud enough for him to hear.

'Now, come on, Ellie. Paint over the rabbit and look a little harder at your cabbages. You haven't got the texture of the leaves right at all. They look far too limp.'

I felt limp all day long at school. I didn't really feel like going out with Russell. Nadine was going round to Magda's house and they were going to sort out all their stuff to see what to wear to Big Mac's party. Nadine isn't remotely interested in any of the boys there. She's still dippy about this *Xanadu* fan Ellis who keeps e-mailing her. Still, she said she'd come along to give Magda moral support.

'*I'll* give you moral support, Mags,' I say, a little wounded.

'Yeah, but you'll be sitting in a corner snogging with Russell all night, won't you?'

'No I won't. Well, not all the time. And there'll be dancing—'

'God, does Russell *dance*?' says Nadine.

I give her a very dark look.

'Sorry, sorry!' she says hurriedly.

We are best friends again, but things are still slightly edgy. Every time I catch Nadine looking at me I wonder if she's thinking, FAT FAT FAT.

I've always said I love Magda and Nadine absolutely equally, but I suppose secretly I've always liked Nadine just a teeny weeny bit more, simply because we've known each other since we were four and we've shared so much together. But now I sometimes wonder if maybe Magda is just that little bit nicer. Nadine can be such a bitch at times. And almost *too* wild. I thought she was mad to get involved with Liam. Then there was that time she insisted we go off with those scary guys in their van, when we tried to go to the Claudie concert. And now she's gone truly crazy, confiding all sorts of secret stuff to a total stranger.

I tried having one more go at telling her how risky this can be but she just laughed at me. She's starting to laugh at me more and more now. She acts like I've become Ms Dull and Deadly Boring since going out with Russell. Which is ridiculous. Isn't it?

I didn't have such a great time with Russell last night. I was feeling lousy but he'd set his heart on going to this fantasy film full of men with helmets and bare chests who zap people with one point of their finger. There were hardly any women in it, just a few silly maidens shrieking in see-through nightie things and a token evil old crone who ended up sinking under a sea of snakes. I thought it was DIRE but Russell lapped it up. He got irritated with me when I moaned and sighed and snuffled. He lectured me for ages afterwards, telling me about this cult comic strip the film was based on.

'You should take an interest, Ellie, seeing as you want to do illustration when you're older. Graphic novels are where it's all happening. No one wants twee little picture books about girly mice.'

I was so insulted – on my mum's behalf as well as mine – that I marched off without even giving him a kiss goodnight. Not that he'd have wanted one anyway. My lips are all chapped and my nose is red and very runny, enough to douse the desire of even the most impassioned boyfriend. Which Russell *is*.

I just don't get boys. One minute he's looking down on me, lecturing me about everything, expecting me to tell him he's wonderful. The next minute he's looking up to me, treating me like the most amazingly exciting girl in the world just because I have two breasts, appendages stuck on the front of half the world's population, for God's sake.

I wish he could be a real *friend*, like Magda and Nadine. Though Nadine isn't always a *friendly* friend now. She's always been a bit moody, right from when she was little. Thank goodness Magda is always happy-go-lucky and fun to be with. She can go on about boys and make-up and clothes a bit *too* much, but basically you couldn't get a better friend.

She brought me some of her mum's special lime cheesecake yesterday to cheer me up. I protested feebly about the mega-million calorie content.

'It's *lime*, Ellie. Lots of vitamin C. Very very good for colds. This cake is *medicinal*, so blow the calories.'

So I did. I must admit I felt a lot better with a tummy full of cheesecake. Magda's mum is such a brilliant cook. Anna used to be OK, but for the last couple of months she hasn't really cooked anything, just heated stuff in the microwave. Still, how can she spend time cooking now she's so busy with her designing? It's OK for Magda's mum. She runs the restaurant with Magda's dad. Cooking is part of her career, so there's no conflict.

There's still every kind of conflict between Dad and Anna. I can hear them downstairs at breakfast now, and Eggs is yelling too.

I'm not getting up. I *can't* get up. I'm too ill. Much much much too ill.

I pull the duvet over my head and curl up in my dark little lair, breathing heavily. I'm having a little doze when there's a knock on the door. I peek out of the duvet. It's Anna with a tray: orange juice, coffee and a croissant and a little bunch of grapes.

'For the invalid,' says Anna.

'You're a darling,' I say thickly, sitting up and rubbing my eyes. There's a letter on the tray too. 'What's that?'

'Isn't it Russell's handwriting?'

'No, his is more twirly.' I open the envelope. I unfold the letter. I find my glasses. I read the letter. By the time I get to the end, the sheet of paper is vibrating because I'm trembling so much.

It's only from Nicola Sharp, the brilliant illustrator who does all those funny Funky Fairy picture books! I used to have a full set of all the Rainbow series. When I was four I thought Ultra-Violet the coolest little fairy ever and wanted all my clothes to be purple, right down to my socks and knickers.

Dear Eleanor Allard,

I'm one of the judges in the children's cartoon competition. I have to make it plain straight away that you *haven't* won – we haven't even had our final judges' meeting yet. And I'm afraid your entry can't be short-listed because it arrived a week after the closing date, without an entry form. Now *I* don't think this matters in the slightest, but the company sponsoring the competition is being incredibly strict about this and insists your entry (and a host of other latecomers too) must be declared ineligible.

Normally I'd just think this is a shame and forget about it, but I can't forget you or your Myrtle Mouse. I see *lots* of children's and young people's artwork, some of it very very good – but I can honestly say your Myrtle is outstandingly original. I'd be proud to have invented her myself.

You are going to *have* to be an illustrator when you grow up!

With every warm wish,

Nicola Sharp

I give such a shriek that Anna shakes my breakfast tray and spills the coffee. 'Ellie, darling, what is it?'

'Oh, Anna!' I say – and I burst into tears.

Dad and Eggs come running in. 'What's happened? Have you scalded yourself, Ellie?' Dad yells.

Anna puts the tray down. She looks at the letter and then flings her arms round me. 'You *clever* girl! Look what Nicola Sharp's written about our Ellie!' she says, thrusting the letter at Dad.

'Nicola Sharp! She's the lady who makes up the Raspberry Red Fairy, the one who blows lots of raspberries,' says Eggs, demonstrating in case we might not understand.

Dad's asking questions, Anna's laughing, I'm crying, Eggs is blowing raspberries, all of us squashed into my tiny bedroom. It's as if we're a proper happy family again, us four Allards together – but then Dad has to spoil it. He's shaking his head as he reads the letter.

'Well done, Ellie,' he says flatly.

'Well done? Is that all you can say?' says Anna. 'Come on, it's wonderful! It's simply amazing that Nicola Sharp picked Ellie's entry out of hundreds, maybe even thousands! Fancy her saying she wishes she'd invented your Myrtle Mouse herself!'

'But she's not Ellie's Myrtle Mouse,' says Dad. 'Ros invented her.'

There's a little silence. Dad rarely talks about my mum, especially not by name. He gives a sad softness to the one syllable. Anna flinches.

I stare at Dad. I feel as if he's snatched all my happiness away. My flu floods back. I hurt all over.

'But Ellie's made Myrtle Mouse her own, you know that!' Anna says sharply.

Dad is looking down at Nicola Sharp's letter. He quotes one word: 'Original.'

It's enough. I know Dad's right . . . in a way.

Anna argues fiercely that he's wrong wrong wrong.

'I know you have huge problems with my silly old sweaters becoming a success, but I'm *amazed* you're not even big enough to be pleased that your own daughter is so talented.'

Dad sucks in his breath. Anna is so angry, breathing hard, red in the face. Eggs is frightened. He slips his hand in mine. I squeeze it tightly, needing to hang onto him for my own sake.

It's all spoilt. Dad's right. I *didn't* invent Myrtle. But it *felt* as if I did.

I need to talk about it. I phone Magda. I wait for

quite a while before I try her, because Magda likes
to sleep late at weekends. Well, she likes to sleep late
every single day but her mum generally unwinds
her from her duvet in time to get to school. I wait
until twelve, when I feel there's a reasonable chance
of finding Magda up and alert.

I've waited too long. She's already gone out.

'I think she's round at Nadine's, Ellie,' says
Magda's mum.

'Oh. Right. Fine.'

'Why don't you pop round to Nadine's too,
dear?'

Why don't I? Because they haven't invited me.
Why didn't they tell me they were seeing each
other on Saturday morning? We always meet up
together. But now together seems to mean
*two*gether. Magda and Nadine have formed a
special exclusive twosome behind my back.

I *could* just slope round to Nadine's . . . But what
if they look at each other and whisper together and
act like I'm a gross intruder?

I can't stand it. It's all happening so quickly. They
don't seem to count me in any more.

Well, to hell with them. I know who really cares
about me. The one who loves me more than anyone else.

I finger my ring and phone Russell.

Chapter Twelv

Girls cry when

their boyfriends
betray them

Twelve
Girls cry when their boyfriends betray them

This party is a *big* mistake. I can't stick Big Mac for a start. He *is* big, a large foul-mouthed strutting lout. He's big-headed too, bragging all over the place. I suppose in material terms he's got a lot to brag about. His house is huge, a four-storeyed Georgian house that's more like a mini-mansion. It's incredibly furnished too. I feel like I've stepped into *Interiors* magazine.

Big Mac's mum and dad disappear pretty early on in the evening. I just hope no one stubs out their roll-up on the Chinese porcelain or pukes on the Turkish carpet. There seems every chance as there's unlimited drink. I thought there might be a weak fruit punch and a few cans of lager, but there are bottles of vodka all over the place and the guys are already knocking the clear liquid back as if it was Perrier water. They mostly *are* guys too. There are a couple of little girls plastered in make-up, teetering on high heels. If you scrubbed their faces you'd see that they're probably still at *primary* school. They're obviously little sisters, desperate not to miss out on a party. The few girls my age divide sharply into two categories – scary girls with tiny tops showing off their navel rings, knocking back the vodka with more aplomb than the boys, and sad girls straight out of the 1950s wearing ladylike party frocks.

I think Magda and Nadine are going to be mad at me for suggesting they come. Still, I'm mad at them for meeting up without me.

I'm mad at Russell too. I'm crammed into an armchair with him, his arm round me, like he's showing me off to all his mates. The Girlfriend. Not that he's acting proud of me. I tried so hard getting ready for the party. I selected and tried on and then rejected three quarters of the clothes in my wardrobe. I even ransacked Anna's wardrobe and tried on this loose crimson velvet dress. Well, it's loose on Anna, and horribly tight on me. And maybe a bit *too* dressy.

I decided it wasn't cool to look as if I'd tried too hard, so I eventually chose this big soft sweater. It's *not* one of Anna's designs, it's plain black with a deep v-neck that shows a little cleavage. A little too much cleavage, actually, so I'm wearing a little black vest thingy underneath. I'm squeezed into my black jeans. They're getting tighter every time I put them on but they do still do up, just. I've got my black pointy boots too, which are already pinching quite a bit, but I daren't kick them off in case my feet smell sweaty.

I don't think I look too bad, especially considering I've still got this filthy cold – but Russell didn't look enthusiastic when he saw me.

'Hi, Ellie. Aren't you changed yet?'

'Yes, I am changed,' I said a little sharply.

'Right. OK. Let's go then.' He fidgeted with his shirt collar.

'Is that a new shirt, Russell? It looks great.' It was OK*ish* – a silky navy affair, just a tad too slick and sleazy for my taste, but I was trying to be generous.

'Cynthia gave it to me,' Russell murmured, wriggling inside it. 'I think it's a bit naff.'

'No, it's lovely,' I said.

I waited.

'Do you think I look OK?'

'What? Yeah. Fine.' He clearly wasn't impressed.

'You don't think I'm a bit . . . understated?' I asked. I wanted reassurance. I didn't get it.

'Well, it *is* a party. Maybe you could change into something a bit more . . . sparkly?'

I felt like kicking him. 'I don't do sparkly, Russell,' I said. 'What do you suggest? A tinsel bikini and a tiara?'

'OK, no need to get shirty. I just thought . . . maybe a skirt? And high heels, you know, to show your legs off a bit? Oh forget it. Come on, let's go.'

I still waited.

'*What?*'

'Don't you want to see my letter from Nicola Sharp?'

'Well, you read it out to me on the phone.

Congratulations.' He kissed me very briefly on my cheek, the way you peck an old auntie.

I can't *believe* this. I expected Russell to be really thrilled for me. He hardly said anything when I told him about it on the phone. He didn't even do a Dad and point out that Myrtle isn't all mine and can't really count as my original creation. When I eventually ran out of steam he just said, 'That's great, Ellie,' very off-hand, like it was the least great thing in the world. But if *he'd* had a personal letter of praise and encouragement from Nicola Sharp he'd be thrilled.

I'd be thrilled for him. And it isn't as if I've won the competition. Russell could still win it himself.

'You wait, Russell, I bet you *do* win the competition,' I whisper, snuggling up to him, trying to act sweet to him in front of his friends.

'Do you have to be so patronizing, Ellie?' Russell hisses. 'Just shut up about it, eh?'

He bends forward and kisses me roughly, his tongue right down my throat. There are raucous cheers and jeers in the background. I struggle free, outraged.

'Don't pull away from me, Ellie,' Russell whispers.

'You do that again and I'll bite your tongue off! Don't think you can insult me one second and slurp all over me the next just to impress your stupid friends.' I'm whispering so they can't hear – but my body language speaks for me.

'Uh-oh! Looks like the little lovebirds are having a tiff!' Big Mac yells. He makes silly noises and suggestions.

'Oh grow up, can't you?' I say.

I wriggle out of the armchair and go and get myself a drink. A vodka. It's the first time I've ever had vodka actually. I approach it very gingerly. It doesn't taste too bad at all, especially with tonic. It doesn't really seem to *have* a taste. I drink it down quickly and try another.

I know this isn't wise but I don't care. I'm not going to sit back down with Russell, not till he shows he's sorry. This doesn't seem likely. He's pointedly ignoring me, swapping stupid dirty jokes with Big Mac and his mates. They all crack up laughing. They are so *childish*. Maybe Nadine is right about going out with schoolboys.

It doesn't look as if Nadine and Magda are coming. I can't say that I blame them. No, wait! I can hear their voices in the hall and Nadine's silver bangles jangling. They walk into the living room — and there's a chorus of wolf whistles. They both go pink, though they struggle madly to act cool. They both look fabulous. Nadine's in a tight black lace top and a weird asymmetric skirt and very high buckled boots with witchy toes. Magda's in a red off-the-shoulder sweater and a very short shiny black skirt, black fishnet tights and black stilettos.

'They're *Ellie's* friends?' says Big Mac, sounding incredulous. 'You pulled the wrong girl out of that little gang, Russell!'

I feel myself going fiery red and pour another drink to help me calm down. Russell doesn't say a word in my defence. He's probably thinking the same as Big Mac.

Well, to hell with him. Maybe *I* picked the

wrong boy. All these boys are awful. I'll simply join up with Nadine and Magda and we'll have a great girly time together.

Only it doesn't work out like that. Magda and Nadine are *surrounded* by boys, Big Mac way to the fore. I'm kind of on the edge, trying to jump up and talk over people's shoulders. They don't even hear me at first, so I speak up a bit. The CD that's playing suddenly stops and I find I'm bellowing in a hushed room. Everyone stares at me like I'm a loony.

'Are you all right, Ellie?' Magda whispers, shoving her way through the adoring throng and pulling me to one side.

'You're bright red in the face,' says Nadine, joining us. 'And your eyes look all weird. Ellie, are you *drunk?*'

'No. Well. I've just had one drink. Well, maybe two.' I hold up my vodka glass. It seems to have a life of its own and spills all over the place, up my drab woolly sleeve and down my dull jeans.

'That's vodka,' says Nadine. She raises her eyebrows. 'And I think you've had more than two, Ellie. Better watch it.'

How can *Nadine* tell me off for drinking! 'You shut up, Nads.'

'You're slurring your words, Ellie!' says Magda.

'No I'm not! Will you two quit getting at me. Come on, let's dance, eh?'

'What about Russell?' says Magda, glancing at him. He's glowering in the armchair, knocking back the vodka too.

'What about him?' I say. 'He doesn't own me,

126

lock, stock and barrel and dancing rights. He doesn't like dancing anyway.'

This is true. He likes anything slow and smoochy, when you just stand and sway together, but anything fast and wild is out of the question. If I really *make* him he'll have a go, but he flings his arms around windmill fashion and looks such a total plonker it's dead embarrassing. I never ever want him to dance in front of Nadine and Magda. Their eyebrows would disappear right up under their hair.

I'm not that great at dancing either. I'm OK. I can keep to the beat and I don't flop around too much. I've practised little routines in the mirror that look passably spontaneous but cool. I'm a novice compared with the others, though.

Nadine is the most *striking* dancer. She does weird gothic things, her face utterly deadpan like she's just risen from the grave, but she puts her hands on her totally flat stomach and kind of wiggles in a way that's incredibly sexy. But not as sexy as Magda. She's gone to dancing classes since she was three, for God's sake, so she's brilliant at any kind of step. It's not just the way she dances anyway, it's the way she looks. She *preens*, looking down and then suddenly looking up under her eyelashes. She tosses her hair and shakes her hips and sticks out her bum and looks incredible. If *I* fluttered my eyelashes and tossed my wild curls and waggled my great big fat bum everyone would laugh.

I don't feel like laughing. I feel like crying. I'm with Magda and Nadine but I feel *separate* from them. I feel separate from myself too. It's like I've stepped aside and I'm staring at this sad fat girl who is everyone's third choice. Russell is watching me gloomily. That's what he's thinking too.

Looks aren't everything. I know that, we all know that. When the music stops I'll tell Naddie and Mags all about Nicola Sharp and how she loves my Myrtle Mouse. No, that makes me feel bad too, like I stole her from my mum. I miss her so terribly. I don't want to keep missing her like this, it hurts too much.

I swig several mouthfuls of vodka straight from the bottle. It doesn't make me feel better. It makes me feel a lot worse. Oh God, I've got to get to the bathroom. I don't know where it is. The room is rushing round and round. I can't see which way to go. I've got to get out or I'll throw up in front of everyone . . .

'Ellie?' Russell had got hold of me. He's pulling me – too hard, so that I stumble. Then Magda has me firmly under one arm, Nadine the other, and they're rushing me out of the room.

'Leave her to us, Russell.'

They get me to a loo in time and stand guard outside the door. When I've stopped being sick at long last they wipe my face and give me a sip of water and take me to a bedroom – dear God, I hope it isn't Big Mac's – and they lie me down and put coats over me because I'm shivering.

'You just close your eyes and go to sleep, Ellie.'

'Yeah, sleep it off, and then you'll feel much better.'

'You're both being so sweet to me now. You do still like me, don't you?' I burble pathetically.

Magda smoothes my hair and Nadine tucks me up. They say they love me and they're my best friends. And they are, they are, they are.

Russell is my boyfriend. He's supposed to look after me. He gave me my ring. But where is he now? He doesn't care about me. Girlfriends are the only ones who are there for you, no matter what. They're the only ones you can trust . . .

I doze off. Some time later someone pulls at my coat-covers. I groan and clutch at them.

'Give over, Ellie. I want my coat!' Nadine whispers. 'I'm going home. This is a crap party. I'm sick of silly schoolboys.'

'What about Mags?' I mumble.

'Oh, she's staying. She seems to be enjoying herself,' says Nadine. She sounds strange. 'I think you'd better go back to sleep, Ellie.'

She leans close and gives me a hug. I'm so glad we're still friends. Still, she's not staying. Magda's the friend waiting for me, looking out for me. She'll help me home if things still aren't right with Russell and me.

I swivel his ring agitatedly round and round my finger, trying to make sense of things. Maybe I was a tiny bit tactless? He's only human. Of course he's going to feel a little bit jealous. Maybe I'll go and try to make it up with him. He's been mean to me, but I haven't exactly behaved sensibly this evening.

Oh God, my head. The minute I try to get off the bed a thumping pain knocks me back. I feel sick again. I am never ever ever going to drink another drop of vodka in my life.

I lie very still, clutching the edge of the bed

because the room is hurtling round and round now. My stomach lurches. Oh no!

I struggle off the bed and feel my way to the door. I bolt along the landing, tripping over intensely twined couples. I make it to the bathroom just in time. Someone else has been ill before me and made a disgusting mess. I hope no one thinks it's me.

I manage to be neatly sick down the loo but my hair flops wildly in the way. I'm terrified I've got sick in it. I end up dunking my head in the wash-basin, rinsing my hair. I'm soaking wet all over but at least I feel a little less fuddled. I towel myself as dry as I can get, shivering violently. I hope I can find my own coat in the pile. I need it anyway. I'm going home. Yes, with Russell and Magda. I've got to find them.

I emerge shakily from the bathroom. Someone's been banging on the door for the last five minutes.

'For God's sake, what were you doing in there, having a bath?' some boy demands. He blinks at my wet hair. 'You *were* having a bath. Weird!'

I push past him and go in search of Magda and Russell. I have to pick my way very carefully along the landing. There are couples huddled all over the place. I don't think they'd like it if I switched the lights on. Maybe more girls turned up while I was upstairs. It looks like Big Mac and a lot of his pals got lucky.

I can dimly make out a couple kissing passion-ately on the stairs. They're lying sideways so I'm going to have to climb right over them.

'Excuse me!' I say, clambering past. My boot

accidentally steps on a hand and there's a groan.

'Oh, sorry—' I start. And then I stop.

I know that voice. I know that hand.

It's Russell.

My boyfriend Russell is lying down with a girl and kissing her.

I feel as if the cold water tap is still running over my head. I stand still. He stays still too, frozen.

The girl doesn't realize I'm here. She nestles closer to him. Then she gives him a little shake. 'Hey, you! Russell! Have you gone to sleep?'

Oh God.

I can't believe it.

It's Magda.

Chapter Thirteen

Girls cry when

their hearts
are breaking,
breaking, breaking

Thirteen
Girls cry when their hearts are breaking, breaking, breaking

I stumble over them and push my way down the stairs. Russell calls after me. I hear Magda say, 'Oh God oh God oh God.'

I elbow my way through the crowd of drunken idiots to the front door. I'm a drunken idiot too. The fresh air outside makes me reel, I can barely stand, but I have to run. I'm terrified they'll come after me and if I have to see them, talk to them, I shall die.

I'm dying now.

Oh, Magda.

You're my *friend*.

How could you? How could you kiss him like that? How could you lie with my boyfriend when you've heard me going on about Russell and how much I love him for weeks and weeks and weeks.

Oh, Russell.

You're my *boyfriend*.

How could you kiss Magda after all our times together, all the things you've whispered and promised, all the things we've done? And to choose Magda of all people, my best friend.

Nadine knew. That's why she went. She wouldn't be part of it. Russell and Magda. After all those things he's said about her. He's gone on about her showiness, practically calling her tarty. Maybe he's secretly fancied her all along.

Oh God, it was all his idea to invite her to the party. Maybe this was exactly what he was hoping for. And I played into his hands by getting drunk. I'm still drunk now, stumbling along in the dark. I have no clear idea where I'm going. I have no ideas at all. I'm just shrieking inside with the shock of it. I can't keep it all inside. I'm making little moaning noises. A woman walking her dog looks at me strangely under the lamplight and asks if I'm all right. I say yes, even though the tears are pouring down my face and it's obvious my heart is breaking.

I thought Russell truly loved me. I thought he wanted me, not Magda. He gave me the ring. The stupid childish freebie ring. I feel for it and yank it off, clumsily, hurting my finger. I throw it with all my strength so that it flies right across the road and disappears into the darkness.

I wish I could disappear too. I can't bear being me. I can't stand it that nothing's worked out for me. Everything's gone wrong. I haven't got anything to cling onto any more. Even Dad doesn't care about me now. He seems all set to walk out on

Anna and Eggs and me. I can't feel good about my Art any more because I'm not original. I haven't got Russell any more. He can't ever have loved me properly or he wouldn't have betrayed me. And worse worse worst of all, I haven't got my girl-friends any more. Nadine's gone off me anyway and Magda . . . Oh, Magda Magda Magda, how could you?

I'm sobbing so much I can't see. I'm in the middle of town now and I keep barging into people and they say stuff but I take no notice. I bolt away from all of them, out into the road. A car brakes and someone screams, 'What are you trying to do, kill yourself?'

I cry harder and someone else says, 'Stupid kid.'

'You think you've got troubles, darling – well, you don't know you're born.' This sad smelly vagrant lurches against me, his dog nipping at my ankles.

I cry harder, trying to push the dog's head away. Then suddenly someone has me firmly by the arm and is telling the vagrant to push off and take his flea-bitten dog with him.

I know this voice. I open my eyes. There's my Mr Wonderful Dream Man, his arm round me, looking concerned.

'It's my little schoolgirl!' he says, astonished.

'*Your* schoolgirl?' one of his pals says, laughing.

'The silly little kid's drunk,' another friend says. 'Leave her alone, Kev, she's trouble.'

I can't believe someone as wonderful as him can possibly be called *Kevin*. But he is, and he *is* wonderful too. He leaves all his friends to go off clubbing without him and finds a taxi and insists on taking me all the way home. I cry that I don't think I've got enough money on me. He insists he's got loads. So then I cry because he's being so kind. He says it's fun acting like Prince Charming, helping damsels in distress. I cry because he's been my Mr Wonderful Prince Charming ever since I started in Year Nine. He gently tells me that he's very flattered, but actually he's gay. I cry because I know that, and up until today I didn't mind too much because I had my own boyfriend, but now I've found him at this party kissing my best friend.

He puts his arms right round me and strokes my still damp hair and tells me that there's no cure for this one. It's going to hurt like hell for a long time but if it's any consolation nearly everyone has to go through this when they're fourteen or fifteen. I'm just a tiny bit thrilled because I'm still only thirteen and he must think I look a little older and, gay or straight, it's fantastic to have a really handsome guy with his arms round me, stroking my hair. But then I think about Magda and Russell and I start sobbing again and I sob and sob until we get home.

He tells the taxi to wait and then he helps me up the drive and knocks on the door. Dad comes out in his dressing gown and stares at me in alarm. I think he's going to start blaming my Mr Dream Man for my condition so I start burbling about his coming to my rescue. Mercifully Dad cottons on and thanks him and then Mr Dream Man (I *can't* call him Kev) kisses me on the forehead and says he'll look out for me and that he hopes I'll feel better soon.

It's so sweet of him – though I'll never ever feel better. Nothing in this whole world can ever make me feel happy again.

When I'm indoors Dad begs me to tell him exactly what's happened. I can't bear to talk about it but Dad won't quit asking me stuff. Anna comes downstairs and I just have to whisper three words – Russell and Magda. She puts her arms round me and rocks me as if I'm as young as Eggs.

'Poor little Ellie,' Dad says, patting my shoulders. 'Still, Russell's not the only boy in the world. I've actually always thought he's a bit of a pompous git, but there you go—'

'Shut up,' says Anna fiercely. 'It's not just the Russell thing. It's because it's Russell and *Magda*.'

Russell and Magda, Russell and Magda, Russell and Magda. Will he start going out with Magda now? Will he meet her after school? Will he take her on our special walks and do all our special things? Will he give Magda a ring too?

I go over it endlessly after Anna puts me to bed. I'm back at the party, stumbling towards the stairs, and then I see them together, Russell and Magda, rewinding throughout the night . . .

The phone rings and I sit up in bed, my heart thumping. I hear Dad's voice sleepily answering. Then he sounds angry. 'Yes, she has got home safely, no thanks to you. No, you can't talk to her. It's the middle of the night. She's fast asleep and I'm certainly not disturbing her. Goodnight.'

I start crying again, my hands over my mouth and nose to muffle it. I hope Dad thinks I'm really asleep, but a minute later I hear footsteps.

There's a whisper outside my door. 'Ellie? Ellie, are you still awake? Can I come in?'

I don't answer but Dad comes in anyway. I'm crying too much to protest.

'Oh, darling.' Dad sits on the end of my bed and scoops me up in a big bear hug. Even though he's been so mean recently I can't help hugging him back.

'Oh, Dad, I'm so unhappy,' I sob.

'I know, Ellie, I know.' Dad holds me tight.

'You *don't* know, Dad. It hurts so.'

'I do know. I hurt too,' says Dad.

It's as if we're back in the past and Mum's just died and all we can do is cling together for comfort.

'Was that Russell on the phone?'

'Yes. Anna says I should have asked you if you wanted to speak to him.'

'No, I didn't!'

'That's what I thought. But maybe I should have asked. I don't seem to know how to get on with you nowadays, Ellie.'

'Or with Anna.'

Dad stiffens, but I feel him nod, his beard brushing against my forehead. 'Or Anna,' he repeats.

'Dad, you and Anna — you're not breaking up, are you?' I whisper against his chest.

'No! No, of course not. Why, Anna hasn't said we are, has she?'

'No, but you both get at each other all the time and you keep staying out late.'

'Yes, well, Anna and I will sort things out, don't worry,' Dad says gruffly.

'Dad, when you stay out late—?'

'Look, Ellie, never you mind about me. Let's think about you. I feel very very sorry for you, but I'm cross too, because you've obviously been drinking quite a lot. I don't really mind if you try half a lager or a few sips of wine, but surely you must realize it's crazy to start on spirits. You could make yourself really ill, even end up in hospital . . .'

Dad drones on and on while I sob weakly. What do I care about drink? I'm never going to a party ever again. I'm not going to go anywhere. Oh God, what am I going to do about school? How can I ever bear to see Magda again?

She phones the next morning. Dad answers and says I'm still asleep. Magda phones again after lunch. Anna answers this time and eventually says, 'Ellie doesn't *want* to talk to you just now, Magda.'

Magda doesn't seem to get the message. There's a knock on the front door just as we're sitting down to tea. It's Magda's special knock, three long raps and then two quick ones, like a little fanfare announcing her arrival.

I groan and get up. 'Anna, it's Magda. Please, tell her to go *away*.'

'Don't you think it might be a good idea to talk things through with her?' Dad suggests. 'Maybe you ought to hear her side of things, Ellie. You don't want to break friends altogether over this, do you?'

'Oh, Dad, I can't *ever* be friends with Magda now,' I say, and I rush upstairs to my room.

I lean against the door and put loud music on to drown out the sound of Magda downstairs. I wait and wait and wait. And then eventually Anna comes and knocks on the door.

'It's me, Ellie. It's OK, Magda's gone. She's so upset. She's desperate to try to explain. She kept on to me about her hamster.'

'*What?* Oh, for goodness' sake!' A wave of fury dries my tears. 'Does Magda think that just because her stupid hamster died that's a perfectly adequate excuse to snog my boyfriend?'

'I wish you wouldn't use that word, Ellie,' Anna says gently. 'It sounds so ugly.'

'It *is* ugly. This whole Magda and Russell situation is ugly ugly ugly. I'm never going to speak to either of them ever again.'

I don't want to speak to anyone, not even Anna. I won't come down for my tea. I stay up in my room. I lie on my bed. I sit up and punch my pillow again and again and again. I cry. I sleep. When I wake up I forget just for a second and start thinking happy thoughts about Russell, reaching for my ring – but my finger is bare and I remember that it's all over.

I can't stay hiding in my room for ever.

It's Monday. I have to go to school, even though I've still got my lousy cold.

I take such a long time getting ready that I'm very late. I miss the bus. I don't care. I dawdle, not wanting to bump into Kev again because I'll feel so embarrassed. He was so wonderfully sweet to me but he must think me such an idiot.

I plod very very slowly. I'm so late getting to school that the prefect with the late book has gone

142

off to her own lessons so I miss out on a detention. I couldn't care less one way or the other. School seems so amazingly stupid and petty that I can't be bothered with it. I've half a mind to slope straight out again – but Mrs Henderson comes jogging along the corridor, wielding a big bag of new netballs. She stops short.

'Eleanor Allard! You weren't at Registration. Good heavens, girl, you're spectacularly late today. I'm waiting with bated breath for your excuse.'

I sigh. 'I haven't really got an excuse, Mrs Henderson.'

Mrs Henderson frowns. I wait for her to inflict some kind of ferocious punishment on me. Perhaps she'll bounce her bag of netballs on my head. She's threatened me with worse. But she drops the bag altogether. Several netballs fall out and roll along the corridor. She tuts but she doesn't go after them. She bends close, peering at me.

'What's up, Ellie?' she asks gently.

Oh no. I don't want her to be kind. If she yells and shouts I can stare her out and act like I don't care. But if she's sweet to me I'll collapse. I can already feel tears prickling in my eyes. I can't cry. Not here, not at school.

I swallow hard, trying to stay in control.

'OK, Ellie. I can see you don't really want to talk about it. Don't worry, I'm not going to press you. But can you just tell me if it's trouble at home? Trouble with friends? Trouble with your love life?'

'It's all of them!' I say, sniffing.

'Oh, Ellie,' says Mrs Henderson. 'It's not much fun being thirteen, I know. I remember when—'

But she shakes her head again, thinking better of it. 'No, I'd better not start the true confession lark or you'll tell Magda and Nadine and you'll all have a good laugh at me.'

'I won't tell Magda and Nadine,' I say mournfully. 'We're not friends any more.'

'Oh, come on, Ellie! You three are totally inseparable. They were both very concerned when you weren't at Registration this morning. Don't worry, you'll make friends again soon, just you wait and see. Now off you go — and see if you can manage a little smile, eh?'

I stretch my lips into a sad little smirk and slope off. I'm amazed horrible old Hockeysticks Henderson can be so kind. I wonder what on earth she was like at thirteen! But it was all so different in her day. She can't possibly understand what it's like now. And she's so wrong about Magda and Nadine. I can't ever be friends with them again.

Well, maybe I can still be friends with Nadine. I know we haven't been getting on too well recently, but she did try to be kind to me at the party. OK, she might be crazy enough to get involved with strangers on the Internet but she'd never ever be cruel enough to make out with my boyfriend.

Maybe she left the party early because she hated seeing Magda with Russell. She's probably not talking to Magda now. Perhaps we'll slot back into being our old twosome, Nadine and Ellie . . .

I go into Mrs Madley's English class. Nadine and Magda are cosied up together in a corner, whispering. They are obviously still the best of friends. So that's the way it is.

I have to go and sit with them when Mrs Madley has finished telling me off for being late. Magda starts to whisper whisper whisper to me. I strain as far away from her as my desk will permit, my hand over my ear to show her I'm not listening.

Mrs Madley *is* listening. 'For goodness' sake, Magda, will you be *quiet*! Now can we all concentrate, please. I want your *Jane Eyre* essays to be exemplary. I don't just require coherent literary analysis. I want you to try to imagine what it must feel like to be poor plain little Jane in her mousy governess clothes, positively aching with anguish when she sees pretty, privileged Blanche Ingram flirting with Mr Rochester.'

I can imagine only too painfully. I don't want to write about *Jane Eyre*. I'm in such a state I'm not up to penning a paragraph on Percy the Park Keeper. I see out of the corner of my eye that Magda is busy writing. After a few minutes she shoves a note onto my desk. I look at her.

'Oh, Ellie, please make friends,' she mouths at me.

I almost weaken. But then Magda puts her hands together in a silly praying gesture, whispering, 'Please please please pretty please!' Nadine copies her. They're treating this like a silly joke. It's just a game to them. They're acting as if this is one of our usual silly fights over who ate the last square of chocolate and got called a greedy pig and went off in a huff. They played this little pantomime act then and it worked.

It's not going to work now. I pick up Magda's note. I see words like 'sorry' and 'mistake' and 'drink' and 'crying' and 'kiss'. I see Magda and Russell kissing and I know these words aren't enough. Magda's taken everything away from me. She doesn't even want Russell for herself. She just had to show she can get anyone she fancies.

To hell with her. I don't want her as my friend now. Or Nadine.

I take the letter and tear it in two and drop it on the floor. Magda goes pink and looks at Nadine. I look away, my head in the air. I jump when Mrs Madley shouts.

'Ellie! Don't throw paper on the floor like that!'

'I'm sorry, Mrs Madley. I'll put it in the wastepaper basket, where it belongs.'

I bend down under my desk, retrieve the letter, and scrumple each half into a tight little ball. I walk to the front of the room and throw both of them into the basket, so hard that they practically bounce.

Chapter Fourteen

Girls cry when

they're lonely

Fourteen
Girls cry when they're lonely

So this is it. I don't have any friends. I don't have a boyfriend. I am Ellie the Ever-so-Unpopular, the girl no one likes, the girl no-one wants. Poor sad stupid fat Ellie.

It's so awful.

I keep wanting to burst into tears at school as I sit tensely in lessons, trying to stare straight past Magda and Nadine.

Nadine tries to get me to talk at break. Magda hangs about in the background. I march straight past.

'Ellie! For heaven's sake, stop being so difficult,' Nadine says. 'Look, I know you're mad at us, but we're still your friends, aren't we?'

'No, you're not,' I say.

Magda's heard. She comes nearer. 'Look, I know

you've got every right to be mad at me, Ellie, but you're still friends with Nadine surely?' she says, reasonably enough.

I'm not ready to be reasonable. I hurt too much. 'I don't want to be friends with either of you,' I say.

'Is this just for today, because you're sore about me snogging Russell?' says Magda.

'Not just today. *For ever,*' I say.

'You don't really mean it, Ellie,' says Nadine. 'You just want to make a dramatic stand and get us to beg and plead with you to stay friends.'

I suppose that's exactly what I *do* want but I can't possibly admit that now. 'I do mean it,' I insist. 'You've changed, Nadine. So have you, Magda. This is it. It's over. Finished. OK?'

I stalk off. I hope that they will come running after me even so. I want them to tell me it's not OK. I want Magda to cry buckets – tanks – *swimming pools* – and beg my forgiveness on bended knees. I want Nadine to admit I'm right, that it's crazy to swap sexy secrets with a stranger on the Internet. I want them both to tell me I'm their best friend in all the world and they can't stand the thought of breaking friends with me.

But they don't.

I walk off by myself. I stay by myself all day. Nadine and Magda go round in a little huddle, arm in arm. I keep thinking about the end of school and what I'm going to do then. What if Russell is waiting at the school gate? *Waiting for Magda.*

I decide I'll rush right past him without so much as a glance in his direction.

It's a huge relief to see he's not there. But as I

walk home by myself I start to wonder. Maybe he should have been there? *Why* wasn't he? Is he too gutless? He can't be concerned with hurting my feelings, not after he's spent half of Saturday night on the stairs with his tongue down Magda's throat.

Why did he do it? Why didn't he go out with Magda in the first place? Why did he go out with me and make me fall in love with him?

I feel so *lonely*. One of the Year Eleven girls is walking hand in hand with her boyfriend in front of me. She smiles up at him. He bends forward and gives her a quick kiss. I close my eyes. It hurts too much to look.

I run all the rest of the way home. I have this mad fantasy that Russell might be there, waiting for me. He doesn't really want Magda, he wants me back, he simply didn't want an embarrassing public encounter outside the school in front of everyone, especially not in front of Magda herself.

But he's not waiting at home. No one's home. Anna's seeing some work people and she's taken Eggs with her. I'm all on my own but this time it's awful. I wander round the house restlessly, unable to settle in any room. The house is horribly quiet, so much so that I jump at every creak of the floor-boards and gurgle of the pipes.

I make myself a coffee and nibble at a biscuit – and then another and another. I eat the whole packet, even though I start to feel sick. I wonder for a moment about *making* myself sick, but I clench my fists and bang them together, furious with myself. I'm not going to do that to myself ever again. I don't care if I feel fatter than ever. I'm *not* going to go back on that ridiculous diet. I'm over all that. I don't care if I'm a sad fat lump and Magda is a sexy curvy dreamboat. Well, I *do* care, of course I do, but I can't change me into Magda and if she's what Russell wants then I just have to accept it.

I *can't* accept it. What is he *playing* at? *Why* didn't I talk to him on Sunday when he phoned? At least he could have given me some kind of explanation. I'd have known where I stood.

So why don't I phone him now?

No. Let him phone me.

He did phone me. I wouldn't speak to him. But I could phone him now. He'll be on his own.

Phone him phone him phone him.

I stand in the hall, pacing up and down – and then I do it.

The phone rings and rings and I don't think he's going to pick up, but just as his answerphone starts up he says, 'Hello?'

The answerphone is still talking – and someone else is talking in the background too. They're saying, 'Is it Ellie?'

My heart turns over. It's Magda.

She's gone home with Russell.

Oh God, I can't stand it. I slam the phone down without saying a word. I run up to my room and fling myself on my bed and cry and cry. I can't kid myself any more. It wasn't just a silly drunken kiss at the party. They've started seeing each other.

The phone rings downstairs. Russell must have dialled 1471 and will know it was me. Oh God, *why* did I try to phone him? They'll be having a right laugh at me now. No, they're not like that. I know

152

they're not really hateful. They'll be feeling guilty and worried about me. That's why they're phoning now. They feel *sorry* for me. That's the bit that's really torturing me. I can see them standing together by the phone, shaking their heads, conferring about poor old Ellie and how best not to hurt her feelings . . .

I punch my pillow, hating Magda, hating Russell, hating *myself*.

I feel so scared and sad and lonely. I want my mum. If only she were still alive. I love Anna now, we're just like big sister and little sister, but she's not the same as a real mum. Not *my* mum.

I'd give anything in the whole world for her to be here now, sitting beside me, scooping me up in her arms, rocking me gently and stroking my hair, whispering Myrtle Mouse stories in my ear . . .

I stop crying and go and get my mum's Myrtle Mouse book. Mum's Myrtle is different from *my* Myrtle. Mum's mouse is little and cute and gentle. She's coloured in soft, sweet pastel shades and her stories are soft and sweet too, little tales for toddlers. *My* Myrtle is done in brightly coloured felt tip, vibrant purples and royal blue and moody jade and stinging emerald. Her adventures are equally colourful, big bold melodramas. She's totally different − but I still can't honestly say she's original.

I take Nicola Sharp's wonderful letter and read it through again. I've already read it so many times it's a wonder the ink hasn't faded. I get out my sketch-pad and write my address in my best nearly-italic handwriting. I draw a picture at the top of the page of Myrtle Mouse as an artist, wearing a big smock with a bow and wielding a large paintbrush.

I write to Nicola Sharp, telling her that I was absolutely thrilled to get her letter. I draw Myrtle leaping up in the air over a tiny moon.

I tell her just how much it means to me. I draw Myrtle in bed with the letter clasped to her chest.

Then I tell her I feel terribly guilty. Myrtle hangs her head, her whole body drooping, even her ears and tail. I explain that I based my Myrtle on some stories my mum wrote and illustrated for me long ago. Mum could never develop them herself because she died, so I've taken Myrtle over, but I can't really take the credit for her invention.

I finish by saying I'm very very sorry for wasting her time, and tell her truthfully just how much I love her own illustrations. I draw Myrtle engrossed in a big Nicola Sharp nursery rhyme book, waving to the mice on the 'Hickory Dickory Dock' page. Then I sign my name, stick the page into a big envelope and address it.

Nicola Sharp won't be interested in me now she knows I've just copied my mum but it makes me feel a bit better to tell her the truth.

Most of the time I'm writing the letter and drawing Myrtle I can forget how unhappy I am. I might not be an artist yet but I will be one day. I shall lose myself in my work. I won't bother with boyfriends. I maybe won't even have any new girl-friends either. I shall live all by myself and illustrate all day and create wonderful picture books.

Chapter Fifteen

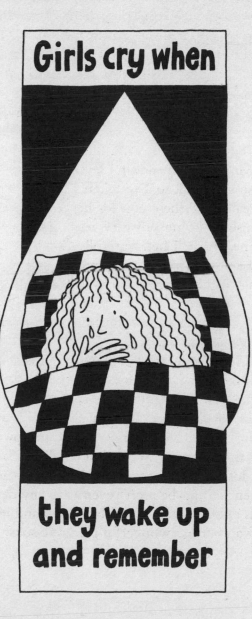

Girls cry when they wake up and remember

Fifteen
Girls cry when they wake up and remember

I can't face school today. My cold is nearly better but I blow my nose constantly and cough into my cornflakes at breakfast.

Dad pats me on the shoulder absent-mindedly. 'You seem a bit droopy, Ellie. Still, you'll soon perk up when you get to school and see Magda and Nadine.' Then he remembers. 'Oh dear, of course. Still, you'll make it up soon, you always do.'

Anna looks at me sympathetically the minute Dad leaves for college. 'He can't seem to help being tactless. Still, he's obviously got other things on his mind.'

I wince at the bitterness of her tone. 'Anna . . . ?'

But she shakes her head slightly and glances at Eggs, who is listlessly making a little cowboy out of the cornflakes packet gallop across the wide prairie of the kitchen table.

I cough again – and again. 'I've got this cough . . .' I say unnecessarily.

Anna sighs, waiting.

'And a pain in my chest. And my head's really hot. I feel totally lousy, honestly.'

'I still think you ought to go to school,' says Anna.

'Oh, please don't make me, Anna. Feel my forehead. I'm sure I've got a temperature. I ache all over. I just want to go back to bed.'

'So do I, Ellie,' says Anna wearily, rubbing her eyes. 'But I just happen to have a mountain of work to see to. I'm supposed to go up to London again but God knows what I'm going to do about Eggs. I daren't ask Nadine's mum again, not after last time.'

'Look, if I don't go to school I can stay in bed this morning and then I'll try to perk up around lunchtime and do some homework and then I'll go and collect Eggs from school for you, OK?'

'It's not one bit OK!' Eggs protests. '*I* had to go to school and my cold was much much worse. I don't want you to meet me, Ellie! I want *you* to meet me, Mum.' His voice is all whiny. He scowls at the cowboy and flicks him over the edge and down down down the Grand Canyon to the kitchen floor.

'Take no notice of him, Anna. He's just trying to manipulate the situation,' I say, retrieving the cowboy and giving him back to Eggs. 'Here we go. The Cornflake Kid bounces back!' I make him do a little twirl. 'Tell you what Eggs, I'll make up a story about him on the way back from school.'

'With lots of fights and shooting?' says Eggs. He's

158

obsessed with guns even though he's not allowed to own a toy one.

'Punch-ups and shoot-outs all over the place,' I promise.

It works. I get to stay at home. I go back to bed, snuggling back under the covers. I hug my pillow because I'm so lonely and my own Ellie Elephant cuddly toy got thrown away long ago. I feel as if I'm on the scrapheap too.

I go back to sleep and have this terrible, stupid dream about Magda and Russell. They're riding along together on a beautiful big white horse with a flowing mane and tail. I'm stuck on this fat little donkey, plodding along in the dust. I try to make it go faster and it suddenly bolts, galloping faster and faster, and I pull on the reins desperately but I can't make it stop. We're getting near the edge of the prairie now and then we're over it and I fall down down down and wake up gasping.

It's so awful waking up and remembering all over again. I have a long private weep, still under the covers, but then I force myself out. I bathe my poor sore eyes in cold water and then make myself some lunch. I actually open up my Maths. I haven't done *two* homeworks now and I don't know what to do. Magda's always helped me out but obviously I can't ask her. I've sometimes rung Russell when I'm stuck but that's an impossibility too. I can see I'm destined to get nought out of twenty for Maths homework from now on.

I read through the first question but I can see there's absolutely no point persevering. I've got a History project and some French verbs to learn but

I can't concentrate on stuff like that either. I end up drawing instead. I want to invent more Myrtle Mouse adventures but I decide I can't do her any more now.

I doodle around on my sketchpad and finally I draw the plastic cowboy and create a Kitchen County world for him. I draw him lassooing beetles and riding bareback on a bucking mouse, but then it occurs to me that this isn't truly original either because I didn't invent the plastic cowboy – he came with the cornflakes. I throw my pencil across the room in despair. Maybe I'm not any good at Art either. All I can do is copy other people.

Still, I've got lots of stories to tell Eggs about the Cornflake Kid on the way home from school. Eggs is reasonably appreciative, skipping along by my side. I'm in the middle of a fresh adventure about the cowboy and a matchbox-on-wheels wagon train when Eggs stops still.

'Are the cowboy's mum and dad on the wagon train?' he asks.

'Well, they *could* be,' I say cautiously.

'He does *have* a mum and dad, doesn't he?'

'Oh yes, definitely.'

'His mum won't die like your mum?'

'No, of course she won't. And *your* mum's not going to die, Eggs.'

'And Dad won't either?'

'No, of course not.'

'But maybe . . . maybe they'll split up? Like, Dad might go and live with someone else?'

'No. Well. Who said he might, Eggs? *Dad* didn't, did he?'

We've both forgotten the cowboy story now. We're back to reality and it's much more scary.

'Dad didn't say. But I heard Mum yelling at him to leave and Dad yelled back that he wanted to.'

'Yeah, but they were just cross. They didn't mean it.' I *hope* they didn't.

'Sam who sits next to me at school says his mum and dad yelled stuff like that and *they* split up. Sam says he bets mine will too.'

'Your mate Sam isn't always right, Eggs. Whereas your big sister Ellie is always always always right.'

'Ellie, did you and Russell yell at each other?'

I stop and swallow hard. 'A bit,' I say. 'Come on, Eggs, let's get home, eh?'

I walk on quickly and Eggs runs to catch up.

'Are you sad, Ellie? Mum said I shouldn't talk about it but I want to *know*.'

'Well, there's nothing to talk about. I am a little bit sad, yes.' Understatement of the entire century!

'Will you get Dan to be your boyfriend again? I liked him best.'

'Absolutely not.'

'I hate all this change stuff and people yelling and splitting,' Eggs says, suddenly near tears.

'I hate it too, Eggs,' I say, reaching for his hand and squeezing it.

I make a big fuss of him when we get home, fixing him special cowboy food for his tea. Well, my approximation of it. I think cowboys eat stuff like buffalo steak and hominy grits (whatever *they* are), but ham steaks and baked beans seem reasonable substitutes.

I'll be eating with Anna later but I can't stop myself snacking on baked beans straight from the saucepan. I'm just wiping up the last of the juice with a slice or two of bread when the door knocker goes. Three long taps and then two short ones – Magda's knock.

'Oh God. We'll pretend we're not in,' I say.

'But we *are* in,' says Eggs.

'Ssh! I don't want them to hear us,' I whisper.

'But that's Magda's knock,' Eggs squeals. 'She's our *friend*!'

He makes a bolt for the door. I'm after him like a shot but I'm not quick enough. Eggs has the front door open while I'm still yelling, 'No! Don't! Will you *listen*, Eggs!'

Magda is standing on the doorstep, biting her lip.

'There! It *is* Magda!' Eggs says triumphantly. 'I *told* you, Ellie. Hey, Magda, come in!'

'Eggs, calm down! Go back to the kitchen and finish your tea,' I say, with as much authority as I can muster.

'*Can* I come in?' Magda asks meekly.

'Of course you can!' says Eggs, laughing, thinking she's joking.

'No, I'm sorry, you can't,' I say.

Eggs laughs more, thinking I'm joking too. Then he sees my face. He's frequently idiotic but he's not stupid. 'Oh, Ellie, have you split up with Magda too?' he says, looking tragic.

'Yes,' I say.

'No,' says Magda. 'Oh, Ellie, you mustn't split up with *anyone*. Especially not Russell. He's nuts about you, you know he is. You should have heard him yesterday going on and on about how he's

162

blown it and how miserable he is.'

'So you did your best to cheer him up, right?' I say.

'Yes. No! Not in that way! I just went round there to see what on earth we could do to make you see sense.'

'It's what the two of you did together on Saturday night that *made* me come to my senses. I never want to speak to either of you ever again. So just go, please.' I try to shut the door but she wedges her shoulder in the way.

'No, Ellie. You've *got* to understand. Look, I know there's no real excuse for what happened, but we were all a bit drunk – *especially* you.'

'Um!' says Eggs, who's been listening, wide-eyed. 'Did you really get drunk, Ellie? Did you fall down? Were you sick?'

'No, of course not,' I lie. 'Now go into the kitchen, Eggs.' I give him a little push to make him go. 'And will you please get out of the way, Magda, so I can close this door.' I give Magda a little push too. A harder one.

'But I need to *explain*.'

'And I told you I'm not *interested*.'

'OK OK, forget me and Russell, though there's truly nothing in it. But I need your help, Ellie.'

I stare at her as if she's gone mad. She steals my girlfriend, she steals my boyfriend – and then she comes round asking for my *help*?

'It's Nadine,' she says. 'It's an emergency. You know this guy Ellis, the Internet one? Well, she's *meeting* him tonight.'

'Then she's stupid.'

'Of course she is.'

'Well, talk her out of it. *You're* her friend.'

'I've tried all day long but she won't listen. She says she has to go. This Ellis says they're showing some special early episodes of *Xanadu* at some cinema in London and Nadine feels she can't miss the chance of seeing them – and him. She's told her mum she's going with us, but obviously she's going on her own and I just don't know what to do. I can't tell on her to her mum, can I? And yet I can't let her go off and meet this Ellis at the cinema, not all by herself. She says she won't *be* by herself, there'll be all the other *Xanadu* fans. Nadine's acting like this is the dream date of the century but I just get this horrible feeling that it's all a bit dodgy. She says I'm paranoid and I'm just jealous because she knows such a fantastic guy. What do you think, Ellie?'

'I think Nadine's mad. Though maybe Ellis *is* fantastic. I don't know. I don't *care*. I'm not friends with Nadine and you any more,' I say.

But I don't really mean it. And Magda knows I don't mean it too.

'Can't we forget all the stuff about you and me and Russell just for tonight, Ellie? Will you come with me to London? I know where they're meeting and at what time. I thought we could maybe get there early and watch out for weird guys and then kind of keep an eye on Nadine. Maybe we could try to sit behind her at the cinema? Though obviously we don't want her to spot us. Look, if you won't go with me I'll go on my own. But the weirdos might home in on me if I'm by myself. Ellie, *will* you come with me? Please? *Please?*'

Chapter Sixteen

Girls cry when

they're sorry

Sixteen
Girls cry when they're sorry

I say yes. What else can I do? I hate Nadine, I hate Magda even more. I never want to be friends with them again. And yet *under* all this I love Nadine, I even love Magda, and I want to be their friend for ever and ever and ever.

It's difficult getting away, though. I tell Anna an elaborate story about making it up with Magda and Nadine. I say we're going to this *Xanadu* showing up in town to celebrate, and fib that Magda's dad is taking us.

Anna folds her arms and shakes her head. 'If you're too sick to go to school you're too sick to go out tonight, Ellie.'

'But you didn't mind one bit about me being sick when you needed me to fetch Eggs from school.'

'Absolutely. I'm all in favour of dramatic re-
coveries when it's to help me do an honest job.
However, I've got a heart of stone when it comes
to nights out with your friends. I thought they were
your deadly enemies now, anyway. Especially
Magda.'

'Well, like I said, we've made it up.'

'There! I *told* you you would,' says Dad, coming
into the kitchen. He gives me a quick hug. I
breathe in his warm oil-painty smell. For once
I don't wriggle away from him.

'Yes, you're nearly always proved right, Dad,' I
say.

Anna raises her eyebrows in disgust, knowing
what's coming. I feel guilty playing such a low-
down trick but this is an *emergency*.

'Dad, Magda still feels a bit bad about things.
She's talked her dad into taking us up to London
tonight so we can see this special showing of
vintage *Xanadu* episodes. I can go, can't I?'

'Of course you can go,' says Dad.

'I've just said she can't,' says Anna.

'Well, *I've* just said she can,' says Dad.

'Oh, for God's sake! Do you have to fight me
over *everything*?' says Anna, and she burst into tears.

I feel guiltier than ever, but I have to take advan-
tage of the situation. I pull my jacket on, grab my
bag and make a dash for it.

I meet Magda at the station as arranged. She's
wearing her red sweater, short skirt and stiletto
heels and is attracting a lot of attention.

'I thought the entire point of this exercise was us
blurring into the background so we can keep

watch over Nadine without being spotted. Well ha ha. You might as well be walking round with a spotlight on you in that get-up. And suppose they go off for a walk together? You can't walk the length of the road in those silly stilettos. Maybe that's how you came to be lying on the stairs at the party? You simply fell over?'

Magda looks stricken. 'Oh, Ellie, I'm sorry. I forgot I was wearing this outfit on Saturday. Oh God, I feel so dreadful—'

'Good! Because I do too. But let's forget about the party for the moment and get up to London. What are we going to do if Nadine's on the platform? Kid her we're the best of chums going on a girls' night out?'

'She won't be. We're going extra early to avoid her. But . . . *can't* this be a kind of girls' night out? *Please* let's make friends, El. If you'll only let me explain properly—'

'I'm warning you, Magda. Just shut *up* about the bloody party.'

She doesn't. She goes on and on and on about it all the way on the train. I make out I'm not listening. I put my hands over my ears but Magda simply raises her voice. I go and sit in another carriage but she follows me. She sits down beside me and puts her arm through mine, trying to anchor me into my seat.

'I'm going to make you listen if it's the last thing I do,' she says.

'It *will* be the last thing you do because I'm going to throw you right out that window if you dare start talking about you and Russell. Can't you understand? It's too painful,' I say, trying not to cry.

'It's painful for me too, Ellie,' says Magda. She's nearly crying too, her eyes brimming. 'I feel so terrible. I didn't *mean* to. Russell didn't either. It just kind of happened without us realizing.'

'Oh, like there was this extraordinary magnetic force that sucked you both up and hurtled you towards each other and stuck you together, tongue to tongue?'

'It wasn't the fact that it was Russell. It could have been anyone. He just happened to be *there*. It was the same for him. It wasn't *me* he wanted. He doesn't even like me, Ellie, you know that.'

'Yeah, he was acting like you thoroughly repel him on Saturday night.'

'That's all he thinks I'm good for,' says Magda, her face crumpling. 'That's what all the boys think. Look, I was feeling really, really fed up at that party. I know I was laughing and joking but underneath I felt lousy, really *cheap*. I heard all the things they were whispering about good old Magda. Meaning *bad* old Magda. I don't know what to do. I like dressing up and looking sexy and having guys stare at me, of course I do – but they never seem to want to know *me*.

'I tried having a swig of that vodka but it didn't make me feel better, it made me feel worse. I started feeling really sorry for myself. I went to the bathroom and sat on the stairs and had a little weep about it, wondering why all my relationships go wrong. Well, I don't even *have* relationships. Even Greg has gone off me now because I won't go further than kissing. Then I started thinking about little Fudge and what it must have been like for her, having sex for the first time and getting all confused and depressed and running away and then suddenly falling and falling . . . OK, I was pretty maudlin. Then Russell fell over me on his way back from the bathroom and he heard me sobbing. He thought he'd hurt me so he sat down beside me and put his arm round me, just to comfort me. I howled ridiculously about Fudge. He said he hadn't realized I was such a softie at heart and then *he* practically started crying and said some stupid stuff about you and then—'

'What stupid stuff?'

'Oh, you don't want to know. He didn't mean it. He was just a bit drunk—'

'Magda. Tell – me – what – he – said.'

'He said you thought you were absolutely *it* now because this artist lady had written you a letter and how you had a cheek saying he copied you and he'd wanted to be an artist all his life and he couldn't help feeling his artwork is better than yours simply because he's two years older than you and works harder at it and is maybe a bit more naturally talented.'

I say something *incredibly* rude.

'I knew you didn't want to hear,' says Magda.

'He's so *jealous*. It's pathetic,' I say.

'Yeah, well, he's a bloke, isn't he? They don't like it if you're better than them.'

'So, do you think my artwork is better than Russell's?'

'Of course I do! And Russell realizes it is too. That's why he's going on about it so much. Oh,

Ellie, you are dense at times. Anyway, he was bleating on about this, and I was blubbing about my little Fudgypops, practically lying on Russell's chest. I was just using him like a pillow, honestly. But then I moved and he moved and I swear I don't know how − it was pitch-black, remember, so we couldn't see what we were doing − but what we *were* doing was kissing.'

'Stop right there!' I say. And then, 'Why *didn't* you stop right there?'

'I know. If only we had. But it just felt so nice, Ellie, that I couldn't quite bring myself to stop. I thought Greg was a good kisser but your Russell is fantastic.'

'He's not my Russell any more. He's yours.'

'No he's not! He doesn't want me. He's nuts about you, Ellie. He wants you back so badly you could win the wretched Turner Art Prize and he wouldn't care.'

'Well why doesn't he say all this to me?'

'He's been trying to phone you ever since Saturday.'

'Mmm, I suppose he has. But he hasn't come round to see me.'

'I don't think he's got the bottle. Your dad can be a bit scary sometimes.'

'My dad's hardly ever at home at the moment.'

'So if Russell comes round will you talk to him?'

'Yes. No. I don't know.'

I *don't* know. I don't know what to feel, what to think. I don't know whether I want him back or not.

'I'll think about it,' I tell Magda. 'Let's work out

what we're going to do about Nadine right now.'

We think we've got bags of time to set up a good spying position, but we've got to find this cinema first. We've both been to London heaps of times but it's nearly always been with our families and you don't really notice which tubes to take. Mags and I end up whizzing the wrong way on the Northern Line but eventually we get to Leicester Square. After a lot of looking and asking we find the cinema down a little Soho side street.

It's got the right name – but the wrong films. It's showing a selection of sleazy, silly soft porn. There's no mention at all of any special *Xanadu* screening. I take a deep breath and go inside, feeling ever so small and shy. I ask the girl at the desk about *Xanadu* and she looks at me as if I'm mad.

'That's a television series. We wouldn't show something like that. And I'm afraid you can't see any of the films we *are* showing, you're not old enough.'

'Don't worry, I don't *want* to see those films,' I say, and flounce out.

'So he's telling lies to Nadine just to get her to agree to meet him,' says Magda. 'Oh God, Ellie, I'm so glad you're here.' She gives my arm a little squeeze. I squeeze back without thinking.

'So, shall we wait around the corner?' says Magda.

'Let's go in the Starbucks over the road. We'll be able to see the cinema easily from there. We'll see Nadine when she turns up – and him. I wonder what he looks like? Maybe he's been lying about that too?'

'He told Nadine he's dark with big brown eyes and he's quite tall. He's supposed to be a conventional dresser but he says he's got a cheeky kind of look. She's expecting some kind of Robbie Williams lookalike.'

'Nadine is so stupid,' I say.

The words are barely out of my mouth when a truly gorgeous guy of about nineteen walks past our Starbucks window, crosses the road and stands near the cinema.

My mouth is open. So is Magda's.

'Oh God, it must be him!'

'And he *is* just like Robbie Williams!'

'Oh lucky lucky lucky Nadine!'

'Well, he could still be really weird even if he looks gorgeous.'

'He could get weird with me any day of the week,' says Magda.

'And why did he say *Xanadu* was on at the cinema when it isn't?'

'Maybe he just made a mistake. I think he definitely deserves the benefit of the doubt! Look, he's looking at his watch. He's still a good ten minutes early. Oh, come on, Nadine, you can't keep a guy like him waiting.'

But he isn't waiting for Nadine. A beautiful red-haired girl with a fluffy jacket and the tightest jeans comes sauntering up to him. They smile and kiss and then go into the little Chinese restaurant next to the cinema.

Magda and I sigh.

The guys going into the cinema itself are *very* different.

'That one's actually wearing the proverbial dirty raincoat!' I say. 'And look at *that* one. He's all greasy-looking – and so *old*.'

'*They're* not,' says Magda, chuckling.

Two spotty boys with baseball caps are furtively conferring. They jam their baseball caps down low to hide their faces.

'They're trying to look older so they can get in. They're only about our age. Hey, imagine if Ellis turns out to be a schoolboy!'

'Well, he certainly knows a lot of stuff, judging from his e-mails,' I say.

We watch the boys get sent on their way. An old guy with a beard shakes his head at them. He's standing in front of the programme display case, having a good peer at the topless girls.

'Yuck! Look at the way he's stroking his beard! I *hate* beards,' says Magda. 'Uh-oh! Sorry, Ellie. I forgot your dad's got a beard.'

'It's OK. I hate beards too.'

'Still, your dad's an artist. He's got to look the part, hasn't he? All artists have beards.'

'Only the old-fashioned sort. And the thing is, he's not really an artist – I mean, he doesn't ever paint anything himself nowadays—'

I break off. Nadine is walking along the street, hands in her pockets, trying to look dead casual. Her face is whiter than ever and she's peering around anxiously. She looks over the bearded guy's shoulder at the programme. She frowns, looking puzzled.

The old guy with the beard is looking at her – *leering* at her. She's gone a bit over the top with her

Goth look today. Her eyes are outlined in thick black and she's backcombed her hair into a wild explosion. She's clenched in at the waist with a huge black belt with laces and she's wearing lots of little clip-on ear studs and a very long thick chain that dangles almost to her knees.

'Is that a *lavatory* chain?' Magda giggles.

'Xanadu wears one. It's meant to contain the key to her heart.'

'I wonder if Nad thinks this Ellis is the key to *her* heart? Do you think he's going to come?'

'She looks ever so nervous, doesn't she? Hey, I hate the way that sad old bloke is slathering all over her. Oh my God! He's starting to talk to her!'

The old guy is saying a lot to Nadine. She looks shocked.

'What do you think he's *saying*?' Magda asks, outraged.

'Why doesn't she tell him to push off?'

We lean our foreheads against the glass, staring at Nadine. The old guy has edged right up to her. Nadine has her hand over her mouth. He says something else, smiling. Then he puts his hand on her shoulder! Nadine tries to shake it off but he clings to her. She takes a step backwards but he hangs on.

'Come on, Mags!' I say.

'Yeah, we'll rescue her,' Magda says.

We dash out of Starbucks and cross the road.

'Nadine!'

'It's OK, Nadine, we're here!'

Nadine stares at us as if we've just dropped out of the sky. The old guy stares too. He looks startled

176

– but his arm is still round Nadine.

'You get your hands off her!' I say fiercely.

'Yeah, clear off, you dirty old man!' says Magda.

'Now look here, Nadine's my little girlfriend, aren't you, sweetheart?' he says, fondling her in a way that makes me feel sick.

'You're old enough to be her *grandfather*! Leave her alone or we'll tell the police and have you up for child–molesting,' I say.

He looks worried now. He peers at Nadine. 'Tell them, sweetheart,' he says.

'I'll tell *you*,' says Nadine. 'Get lost! Go on, go away. I don't want anything to do with you.'

So he walks away, down the road, round the corner, gone. Nadine bursts into tears.

'Oh, Naddie, don't cry. It's OK, he won't come back now,' I say.

'Don't be cross with us for coming. We were just so worried about you. But we'll make ourselves scarce when Ellis turns up.'

'*He* was Ellis,' Nadine sobs.

'*What?*'

'But he's *ancient*. Ellis is nineteen.'

'He said he'd lopped a few years off his age.'

'A *few*!'

'And he was sure I wouldn't mind going out with him. He said the *Xanadu* showing was cancelled but – but never mind, because I looked so like the real Xanadu it was as if we were in our own little show together—'

'Oh, yuck yuck!'

'I know. He's so *horrible* – and kind of scary.'

'Well, never mind. You don't have to have

177

anything to do with him ever again. And we're here now. We'll look after you.'

'I'm such an idiot,' Nadine sobs. 'I've been so crazy about Ellis. Now it's like that horrible old man has stolen him away. Oh God, you were right all the time, Ellie – and you haven't even said I told you so.'

'Yet!' I say, giving her a hug.

'You're the best friend in all the world,' says Nadine, hugging me back. 'And you are too, Mags.' She looks at us both anxiously. 'So have you two made it up now?'

Magda looks at me.

'Of course,' I say. 'We're all best friends, for ever and ever and ever.'

Chapter Seventeen

Seventeen

Girls cry when everything ends happily ever after

I keep thinking about the old bearded guy. He keeps morphing into someone else. Someone horribly familiar. He's got Dad's beard – and Dad's hair, Dad's eyes, Dad's face. It's like it's my dad leering at Nadine.

'You're ever so quiet, Ellie,' says Magda on the train. 'We *are* friends again, aren't we?'

'Yes.'

'And you'll make it up with Russell too?' says Nadine.

'I'm not sure,' I say. 'It's not just because of the party. It's a whole load of other stuff. I'm totally off men at the moment.'

'Me too,' says Nadine, shuddering.

'Count me out of this one!' says Magda. 'Look, it's still ever so early. Why don't you two come back

181

to my place and we'll watch a video. I think I've even got the *Xanadu* pilot, Nads! We'll snaffle one of my mum's cheesecakes and have a little feast. Then my dad can really run you both home after. Yeah?'

'Great,' says Nadine.

They look at me.

'Well, I'd love to, but—'

'Oh, Ellie, you *are* still all huffy, I knew it!' Magda wails.

'No, I'm not, silly,' I say, giving her a little dig with my elbow. 'It's just – well, there's something else I have to do before I go home.'

'What's more important than having a laugh with your girlfriends?' says Magda. Then Nadine sighs and gives her a nudge. She mouths one word. Magda goes, 'Ooooh!' They both smile at me.

'Right!' says Magda. 'Of course, Ellie. Come round tomorrow instead or the next night or whenever.'

They think I'm going round to Russell's house to make it up with him.

I really don't know if I want to or not. But that's not where I'm going tonight.

I'm going to the Art College.

I'm sick of Dad. I'm going to have it out with him. He keeps coming up with this stupid excuse that he's working late at the college. Of course he's not doing anything of the sort. He's out somewhere with one of his students, I'm sure of it. Someone half his age. He'll be leering at her, looking like that horrible Ellis – and she won't look that much older than Nadine.

I'm going to go to his room myself, prove there's no one there, then confront Dad when he comes home.

So I say goodbye to Magda and Nadine when we get back to our station and hurry off towards the college. It's a bit weird walking along the streets by myself. I keep seeing men lurking in the shadows. I glare at them all, my fists clenched, ready to smack them straight in the face if they try anything on with me. I know I've gone a bit mad and that they're just perfectly ordinary harmless men coming home from work or the pub or simply out for a stroll – but I've started to suspect all men, *especially* my dad.

I march quickly to the college and stare up at the big dark building. I know which is Dad's room, right up at the top. The light isn't on. There! Working late indeed! The whole college is in darkness apart from a light on the first floor, where the studios are. I peer up – and then catch my breath. Dad *is* there! I can just make out his profile as he stands near the window. His head bobs backwards and forwards. It's as if he's looking at someone. Oh God.

He's there in the studio with some girl student. How *can* he? There's poor Anna worrying herself sick at home.

I run through the gates and up to the college entrance. The main doors are locked but there's a side door round the corner for staff and it's still open. I walk in and start trekking along the long corridor. My boots echo eerily in the silent building. I try to tiptoe, as cautious as a burglar. I creep up the first flight of stairs. My heart's pounding. I wonder what on earth I'm playing at. I'm so scared of what I'm going to see. Maybe I should keep out of things after all. No, I'm going to go through with it. I'm going to confront Dad. I don't care how embarrassing and appalling it is. I've got to know. If my dad's little better than some leering old pervert then I've got to face up to it – and make him face up to it too.

I throw open the studio door. Dad gasps. He's on his own! He's standing in front of a canvas, painting. There's a mirror propped up in front of him. He's working on a self-portrait. I've made him jump so much that he's daubed grizzled beard-colour right across his nose.

'Good God, Ellie! Now look what you made me do! You terrified the life out of me. What on earth are you doing here?'

I stare at him, speechless.

'Are you checking up on me?' Dad asks.

'No! Well . . .'

'Ellie, I've told you and told you, I'm not having some secret affair. Chance would be a fine thing at my age, anyway! All my students treat me like some sad old git way past his sell-by date. Which I suppose I am.'

'No you're not, Dad,' I say uncomfortably. 'I'm sorry I made you jump like that. You can scrape off the smudgy bit, can't you?'

'I don't know. Maybe it's an improvement. Me and my new furry nose.'

I go and stand beside Dad and look properly at the portrait. It's good, of course. Dad's always been great at painting, though he hasn't worked properly on anything for ages. He's painted himself with almost painful precision, putting in every line and grey hair. He's emphasized his sagging tummy, his hunched stance, his worn old shoes.

In the portrait he's standing at his easel, painting. He's gazing intently at the picture on the easel. This is a portrait of a very different Dad. He looks much younger, with a trimmed beard and trendy haircut, a flat stomach and stylish black clothes. He seems to be at some art exhibition. Maybe it's his own private view. He's surrounded by admirers. There's Anna, there's me and Eggs, there's a whole flock of pretty leggy girls raising their glasses of champagne to him, there are older men in suits writing in their cheque books, paying a fortune for each painting.

'Oh, Dad,' I say softly.

'Yeah. Sad, isn't it?' says Dad.

'It's – it's a brilliant painting.' But it *is* sad. Dad's obviously all too aware that he hasn't achieved all the things he once longed for.

'It isn't brilliant, Ellie, but it's the best I can do. I've been working on it evening after evening, try-ing so hard. But it's all a bit pointless. I want to be him –' Dad points to the portrait within the portrait – 'but I'm stuck being him. A jealous old idiot.'

'Oh, Dad, I shouldn't ever have said that. I'm so sorry. I didn't really mean it. And I like the real you much much better.'

'Well, I'm glad about that, Ellie, even if you're just being kind to your old dad.'

'Anna likes the real you best too.'

'I'm not so sure about that. She's starting to move in a different world now. I think she's getting pretty fed up with me. Maybe she'll meet some trendy successful designer—'

'Maybe she will. But she won't want him, Dad. She just wants you. I know. She's been going crazy worrying about you. Why didn't you *tell* us you were just working on a painting?'

'I wanted to see if I could do something really worthwhile. I didn't want to tell anyone in case it didn't come off. I needed to keep it to myself.'

'And maybe you kind of *wanted* to make Anna worry?' I suggest.

'She's so busy she doesn't notice if I'm there or not,' says Dad.

'Oh, *Dad*! You know that's not true. Anna needs you so much. She loves you.'

'Well – I love her,' Dad says gruffly.

'Then why don't you just come home and tell her?'

'OK. Home it is. Ellie, do you really think the painting's OK?'

'I told you, Dad. It's wonderful.'

'Well – I suppose it isn't *too* bad. It still needs quite a bit of work on it.'

'Like the hairy nose?'

'I'll sort that in a tick.' Dad dips his brush in pinky beige paint and starts splodging over the brown.

'Hey, Dad, try painting out your beard too. See what you might look like without one.'

'I've always had a beard,' says Dad.

'Like when you were a little boy?'

186

'Absolutely. I had the cutest stubble as a baby, a little goatee as a toddler, and a full beard from when I was six,' says Dad, laughing. 'OK, OK, let's shave it off.'

He deftly paints over his beard. His painted face looks strangely naked, but I think I like it.

'It makes you look much younger, Dad.'

'Do you think so?' says Dad, stroking his real beard. 'Mm. Maybe I'll shave the real one off.'

'See what Anna thinks. Maybe she *likes* the Father Christmas look.'

'Nobody can insult you like your number one daughter,' says Dad.

He gives me a little poke with the end of his paintbrush. I pick up another and we have a mock fencing match. Dad's acting like *Dad* again and it's such a relief.

We go home together. I go straight up to bed and leave Dad and Anna to talk. I don't know if they really will sort things out – but certainly at breakfast next morning they both seem unusually chirpy.

Dad gives Anna a quick kiss on the cheek when he leaves for college. I raise my eyebrows at Anna. She goes a little pink and smiles demurely.

There's a thud of post coming through the letterbox. Eggs runs to fetch it.

'Boring boring boring,' he says, flipping through all the business envelopes and giving them to Anna. 'Why do you get all this post now, Mum?'

'Because of my jumpers, darling. Maybe I'll have to get a PA soon, someone to help answer all the letters. And we'll find a proper lady to look after you after school, Eggs, if I can't be there. I've just got to get myself organized – somehow!' says Anna.

Eggs still has a letter in either hand. 'These are yours, Ellie. It's not fair, *I* want a letter.'

'I'll write you a Cornflake Kid letter after school, OK?' I say. 'Let's see my letters then!'

I take them and look from one to the other, my heart thumping. I recognize the handwriting on both. I don't know which to open first. I juggle them from hand to hand, and then open Nicola Sharp's letter first. I scan the page. She's drawn herself at the end, hand in hand with lots of her rainbow fairies!

Dear Ellie,
Don't worry, I think you're the most original illustrator ever. It's very touching that you've used your mother's mouse designs – but you've moved on and made Myrtle *yours*.

I love all the mousy illustrations in your letter. I'd like to see more of your work. Maybe we can meet up sometime? Perhaps you'd like to spend a day at my studio in the summer holidays? I can show you how to draw rainbow fairies and you can show me how to draw Myrtle Mouse.
With very best wishes,
Nicola

'Oh wow! Nicola Sharp's asked me round to her studio, Anna! She doesn't mind a bit that my mum invented Myrtle. She *still* thinks I'm original.'

188

I hand her the letter. Eggs sees the coloured picture and tries to snatch it.

'Careful, sweetheart,' says Anna. 'This is a very special letter. Look, Nicola Sharp's done a lovely drawing just for Ellie!'

'I think Ellie's drawings are better!' says Eggs. 'Will you draw the Cornflake Kid on my letter, Ellie?'

'Yes, I promise,' I say as I open the other envelope. There's a very large sketchpad page folded up inside.

'Is it from Russell?' says Anna.

'I think so.' I open it out with trembling hands. It's a huge picture of an enormous ring engraved over and over again with the word SORRY, with little hearts and flowers in between each word. It must have taken him hours and hours to draw, and it's been coloured in so carefully too, each flower a different shade, the gold ring beautifully high-lighted, the background a brilliant, even blue.

Underneath, Russell writes:

Darling Ellie,
I'm so sorry sorry sorry sorry sorry sorry sorry sorry sorry sorry sorry. Could we rewind right back and start all over again? I'll be in the McDonald's where we first met straight after school, waiting and waiting and waiting.
Love Russell xxxxxx

'Well?' says Anna. 'Is he sorry enough?'

'I – I think so.'

'And how do you feel about him now?'

'I don't know,' I say.

Anna smiles at me. 'I think you do!' she says and gives me a hug.

I run nearly all the way to school. I turn the corner – and there's my Mr Wonderful Dream Man on his way to work.

'Ellie! I was so hoping to bump into you!'

'Not literally, this time! Kev, thanks so much for looking after me that night. You were so sweet to me. I was in a right state, wasn't I? I'm so sorry!'

'I don't need to ask how you are now. You and the boyfriend are back together again, right?'

'What makes you think that?'

'Because you've got a big smile stretching from ear to ear!'

I stay smiling all day long. Nadine and Magda tease me fondly. I can't *wait* until the end of school. I start haring down the corridor the moment the bell goes.

'Slow down, Ellie, you'll knock the little ones over!' Mrs Henderson calls, coming after me. 'I wish I could make you run that fast on the hockey pitch! Still, I'm very glad you've cheered up.'

I grin at Mrs Henderson. She's really not such a bad old stick after all.

Then I gallop off again. Out of school, into town, round to McDonald's – and there, sitting at a table, is Russell. He's looking around anxiously, his hair tousled, dark circles under his eyes. He's clutching his sketchbook. I want to rush right up to him, but I force myself to saunter slowly past, up to the counter for French fries and Coke.

Then I sit at the table opposite him. I get out my own little notebook. I start drawing in it, taking little nibbles of chips and sips of Coke. I draw Russell. He is busy drawing too. I'm drawing him drawing me and he's drawing me drawing him. Every so often our eyes meet as we look up. I can't help smiling. Russell smiles too. He gets up and comes over to me. It looks like we're starting all over again.

It won't be the same.

It will be different.

It could be *better*.

We'll have to wait and see . . .

ABOUT THE AUTHOR

JACQUELINE WILSON was born in Bath in 1945, but has spent most of her life in Kingston-on-Thames, Surrey. She always wanted to be a writer and wrote her first 'novel' when she was nine, filling countless Woolworths' exercise books as she grew up. She started work at a publishing company and then went on to work as a journalist on *Jackie* magazine (which was named after her) before turning to writing fiction full-time.

Since 1990 Jacqueline has written prolifically for children and has won many of the UK's top awards for children's books, including the Smarties Prize in 2000 and the Guardian Children's Fiction Award and the Children's Book of the Year in 1999. Jacqueline was awarded an OBE in the Queen's Birthday Honours list, in Golden Jubilee Year, 2002.

Over 8 million copies of Jacqueline's books have now been sold in the UK and approximately 50,000 copies of her books are sold each month. An avid reader herself, Jacqueline has a personal collection of more than 10,000 books.

She has one grown-up daughter.

'A brilliant young writer of wit and subtlety whose stories are never patronising and are often complex and many-layered'
THE TIMES

'Jacqueline Wilson has a rare gift for writing lightly and amusingly about emotional issues'
BOOKSELLER

'Wilson writes like a child, and children instantly recognize themselves in her characters. The tone of voice is faultless, her stories are about the problems many children face, and her plots work with classic simplicity... a subtle art is concealed by artlessness, and some might call that genius'
DAILY TELEGRAPH